EARLY PRAISE FOR
40 NICKELS
by R. Daniel Lester

"Action packed from the first sentence, R. Daniel Lester offers readers a briskly paced down-and-out detective yarn, cleverly composed and executed at a machine gun clip. A twisted look at the lengths desperation stretches its victims and the bizarre attempts one man makes to stay one step ahead of his runaway case. Full of kooky phantasmagoric imagery and the blackest diner coffee this side of three A.M. *40 Nickels* is worth every penny."

—**J.D. Graves**, Editor-in-Chief, *Econoclash Revue*

"You're guaranteed to walk into the fight heavy with your knuckles wrapped around 40 Nickels. Fitch is a hard-up dick on a long, strange trip, whose mistress is chaos. Lester's tale takes you right into the back alleys of post-war Vancouver, where you might end up chasing The Sacred Glow, and just when you think you got lucky, daddio, you end up on your back, with a new set of choppers."

—**Scotch Rutherford**, Managing Editor, *Switchblade*

"The thing about R. Daniel Lester's writing is it's boiling just under the surface. You ride along through his stories, enjoying how he has all the right things in all the right amounts. But where you can't see it, tension is rising. Fangs are being bared. It's boiling. And when it gets to the surface, he's got you where his talent wants you when it hits."

—**Ryan Sayles**, author of the *Richard Dean Buckner* thrillers

Also by R. Daniel Lester

DEAD CLOWN BLUES

A CARNEGIE FITCH MYSTERY FIASCO

40 NICKELS

R. DANIEL LESTER

SHOTGUN HONEY

DEAD CLOWN BLUES
Text copyright 2019 R. Daniel Lester.

All rights reserved. This book or any portion thereof may not be reproduced or used in any manner whatsoever without the express written permission of the publisher except for the use of brief quotations in a book review.

This book is a work of fiction. Names, characters, places, and incidents either are products of the author's imagination or are used fictitiously. Any resemblance to actual persons, living or dead, events, or locales is entirely coincidental.

Published by Shotgun Honey, an imprint of Down & Out Books

Shotgun Honey
215 Loma Road
Charleston, WV 25314
www.ShotgunHoney.com

Down & Out Books
3959 Van Dyke Rd, Ste. 265
Lutz, FL 33558
www.DownAndOutBooks.com

Cover Design by Bad Fido.
Author photo by Charles Lester.

First Printing 2019

ISBN-10: 1-948235-16-1
ISBN-13: 978-1-948235-16-7

*This book is dedicated to the void that I battled
with until the last word was written.
Well played. I'll be seeing you again soon, no doubt.*

40 NICKELS

1

Before: Toronto, Ontario, 1956

THE PUNCH KNOCKED THE WIND OUT of me good, a fist right in the breadbasket. I coughed. I wheezed. I sucked air that wasn't there. Then I coughed some more. It was half real and half comedy bit, a little show for the barflies to give me time to recover. Plan my next move. Running away very fast was probably my best option, considering the big oaf didn't seem bothered at all by the barstool I'd cracked over his back. But he was well into a full-on drunk with no signs of stopping until he crossed the finish line so that may have had something to do with it.

Booze logic. The body forgets to feel pain.

I didn't have the luxury because I was practically sober. Spent my last dime on a glass of beer at the Wheat Sheaf Tavern, corner of King and Bathurst, one I was planning to nurse for a good long while. That is, until the large fella something degrading about my hat. And then I said something about his mother and voices were raised and that's when I hit him with the barstool. Best to end a fight before it begins being a personal credo. But it only seemed to rile him up more. I blamed the barstool—lousy, cheap manufacturing. Broke like kindling surrendering in front of a fire.

He towered over me. "So, you got somethin' you wanna say or do you want a knuckle sandwich for lunch?" When I didn't respond right away, his work boot nudged me in the ribs.

"Okay," I said, "I shouldn't have compared your mother to a bottom feeding sucker fish. I don't even know the woman, I'm sure she's lovely."

"Hmm. Apology accepted. Now, you wanna get up or lie on the floor some more?"

I mulled it over. "I suppose I could give upright a shot."

He reached out a giant bear paw and helped pull me up. I stood, straightening up slowly to look him in the eye. No such luck. My gaze ended at his chin, even though I was no slouch in the height department. They built 'em big where this one came from. And that was the problem with starting a fight when the other guy was sitting down—perspective.

"You pack quite a wallop, fella," I said, when the spots in front of my eyes stopped dancing jigs and disappeared.

He nodded, smiled, and placed a tightly wrapped roll of nickels on the counter. "I had a little help."

"That's nifty," I said.

"Always served me pretty well. Makes a point."

"That it does. Though I'm curious: you roll 'em yourself or get 'em from the bank already done?"

"Oh, I roll 'em myself. Figure it's more meaningful that way."

"Sure, I can see that. You from around here?"

"Nah. Passin' through. Headed north to the Sudbury Basin, to work the mine." So that explained all the beer. He was getting one last drunk in before tunneling to the Earth's core to harvest its precious metals.

"Probably for the best. Otherwise I don't think there'd be enough barstools to go around. I'm Carnegie Fitch. But most people just call me Fitch."

"I'm Wendell."

We shook hands like proper gentlemen, despite our deficiencies of character.

"Not such a pleasure to meet you, Wendell, but I suppose I had it coming. So, what do you mine up there, anyway?"

"Nickel and copper, mostly."

"Wait a minute, you mine for nickel *and* carry a roll of nickels? Your commitment to character in this human play called 'Life' is worthy of admiration and praise. You're a true artiste. So much that I'd like to offer you a beer for your efforts. Bartender, a drink for my new friend here." I patted my pockets exaggeratedly. I could do some performance art, too. "But oh yeah, my wallet's a graveyard until payday." The bartender stopped pouring.

Wendell laughed, a loud, hollow sound. "You're a funny guy, Fitch. How 'bout I buy you a beer?"

The bartender finished pouring and placed the beer in front of me, shaking his head in distain. He had no flair for the dramatic, I suppose, no appreciation for the arts. Regardless, it was the fastest beer I ever drank. One big gulp. Wendell was impressed and even offered to spring for another. Every drunk loved a drinking buddy. This time around, I declined. I wanted out of there. I needed air. And, frankly, an escape route. So, I wished him good luck with the mine and said to make friends with a canary. The remark shot over his head even as tall as he was and all I got back for my razor-sharp wit was a blank stare. Fair enough. Brains and brawn didn't necessarily have to travel on the same ticket.

When the door to the tavern shut behind me, I didn't exactly run but I didn't dilly-dally either. I fast walked down

Bathurst to the end of the block, crossed the street, hopped a fence and cut across a deserted lot where only the crabgrass and broken bottles lay, seeking the safety of a network of alleys and back routes leading to the collection of tar paper shacks and hobo tents I called home sweet home. I climbed out the other side of the lot, stopped and put my back against the nearest wall, peering around the corner of the brick building. Nothing to see. So I seemed to be in the clear: no sign of an irate Wendell looking for the asshole that ripped him off for two bucks worth of nickels. Fat city.

The nickels still felt warm from the palm of his sucker punch hand. I dropped the roll in my shirt pocket and began to whistle. No bird song, but as I'd recently graduated from forcing air between pursed lips only to get nothing but a "pfft" sound I enjoyed the few notes I was able to produce. I'd gone into the bar to drink away my last dimes and ended up making two bucks, even if it wasn't completely on the up and up. But neither was slugging a guy in the gut with a roll of nickels.

My "this day really turned itself around" feeling lasted about thirty seconds. Because that was when I heard it: the whistling. Not like my whistling, no, of course not. That wouldn't do. Not for him. He could whistle like a cat could meow. And then there he was, casually leaning in the alcove of a warehouse doorway up the alley from me. Hopping down, still whistling, and approaching with a wolf-like gait, a predator's lope. Only a sniff of prey. Not hunting, not yet. The whistling stopped. He smiled big.

"Mr. Carnegie Fitch, old buddy, old pal, fate has seen fit to once again intertwine our paths," he said, opening his arms like we were long lost friends. Only we were neither.

"Hey, Janssen," I said.

Copernicus Janssen was his handle, the defrocked dentist

from Halifax, Nova Scotia. He'd also, apparently, spent some time in Kingston because some of the Ontario guys called him the "Kingston Kook," though not to his face. Back east, on the coast, story was he'd been chased out of town for being more interested getting blitzed on his own laughing gas supply, especially while patients were in the chair with their pie-holes hanging open. And he'd get his fingers all in their mouths and then begin one of his fiery longwinded rants about whatever was bothering him that day. The man could lay down the ol' talky talk, no doubt. Plus, he could forge a hell of a scrip and knew the good drugs so a lot of my fellow drifters really liked to have him around. Bennies and devils never did it for me—I was more a caffeine and whisky kind of guy.

Janssen got right up to me, like he was apt to do, a professional invader of personal spaces. A few hairs shorter than me, he looked up and grabbed me around the shoulders and kneaded the flesh with powerful fingers in what was probably supposed to be a comforting embrace. It wasn't. Also jarring was his breath. Here we were, living on the edge, in the muck, and he had the nerve to have fresh breath. But it was disturbingly fresh, a cloying peppermint scent that practically seared the inside of my nostrils.

"A splendid morning brings splendid company. Smell that beautiful air, my dear Fitch. Why, there's a butterfly! Good day to you, too!" He removed his hands from my shoulders and crossed one over the other at the thumbs and mimicked a flying butterfly. Same with his breath, no matter how low down he got, and he'd been burrowing down into the soil for several years now, his fingernails were always in perfect condition. Not a hangnail or a dirty, unclipped pinky among them.

"What do you want, Janssen?"

"Want? What should I want, other than to take in this fine morning air, walk this fine Earth and pass the time with fine conversation?"

Right. It was Janssen's world and we were all the players, the saps, the dumb rubes to his slick carny. And "fine conversation" always meant "captive audience for my lengthy, spirited diatribe about the blah blah blah and did I tell you about the blah blah blah." "Uh, no thanks," I said. "Gotta go."

"Excellent, I understand completely. Places to go and people to see."

"Yeah, exactly."

"But it is such a fine morning so why don't I walk with you?" Janssen was determined not to take a hint. I shrugged and walked on. He kept pace. A few weeks back, he'd attached himself to me for a whole day, like a shadow in the desert sun and nowhere to find shade. "So exactly where are we going?"

Bluff called, I had to produce. Think, Fitch, think. Okay, I knew how to scare him off. I put on my best serious face and said, "To look for a job."

He didn't recoil in horror like I'd hoped. "Oh? I thought you'd already taken a position. Why, didn't you storm out of camp a few days ago calling us all degenerate lowlifes and vowing to 'start over,' 'get it right this time' and 'live a normal life?'"

He had me there, I did. Every blue moon the shroud of have-a-career-get-a-bank-account-take-some-responsibility would settle over me and I'd comb the job ads for a suitable opening, vowing to clean up my act once and for all. And I had a gift of the gab when it suited me and could often talk myself up in an interview, enough to get the job anyway. Maintaining it was another thing altogether. Like this last job: office work, 9-5. Basically take paper from that place and move it there. Which was fine now-and-then but every day? And from now until retirement? No thanks.

"I'm taking personal leave," I said.

"Their loss, I'm sure," said Janssen with a knowing grin.

"Undoubtedly," I said, firing a knowing grin back. "But let's stop agreeing, we might get wrinkles from all the smiling."

"Couldn't agree more, good sir, couldn't agree more."

Leave it to Janssen to have to win on a word count, too. He repeated everything. Probably thought it was folksy and inspired trust. Personally, it made me want to throw up but every mark had a different threshold. Because, yes, as it turned out, I was to be the mark that morning, painted with a big bullseye and ripe for the targeting despite my defensive strategy.

"Say, didn't you use to sell encyclopedias while putting yourself through cavity college?" It irked Janssen like nothing else did if you didn't wrap his former profession up in fancy cloths and place it on a golden altar and then bow down in front of it with the appropriate deference. So I made sure to do exactly that whenever possible.

"Well, I learned a sight more than how to fill cavities, let me tell you, Mr. Fitch, but, yes, I did spend several years flogging my volumes of wordy wares, educating the masses to all the wonders the world has to share."

Jeez, a simple "yeah" was never enough for this guy. But I felt the position of the conversational sun changing. If I could get a tall building between it and me, get Janssen onto someone or something else, I might have a chance of losing my annoying shadow. A Janssen distracted was a Janssen disappeared.

"Must've been tough," I said.

Janssen nodded. "There was many a day where my feet were worse for wear. The dogs were barking, as they say."

"Nah, for your mind."

He cocked his head and frowned. "Excuse me?"

"There you were tryin' to fund your way though rotten molar school amongst all them preppy rich kids and you had to bring a knife to a gun battle to survive."

"I don't follow you."

"Books, Janssen. Who reads anymore? It's all about the almighty glow of the television screen. You show up at their house, what were most of them doin'? Watching TV, right?"

"I suppose."

"Sure, maybe an average Joe buys a set of A-Zs to look important but does he actually read them, when the screen can tell him everything he needs to know? TV is the new religion, mark my words."

As we reached the end of the alley, I hope it'd mean we reached the end of the conversation. I got lucky. All of a sudden, Janssen had itchy feet, had to get going. He remembered he had irons in the fire and off he went, whistling a merry tune. Which was reason for me to whistle, too, and I gave my pathetic song a whirl before stopping mid-pfft. Wait a—

No.

No.

It couldn't be.

I patted all my pockets.

Oh, it be.

Janssen, the rotten scoundrel, had lifted my 40 nickels.

2

Now: Vancouver, British Columbia, 1958

TWO OMELETTES ON ORDER, four sunny side up eggs on the grill. Hashbrowns sizzling. Toast down. A short stack of pancakes on the griddle. Organized chaos was the only thing you could call the diner kitchen. It boggled the mind. The short order cook of the modern age was a wizard poet, an alchemist, a master of the dark arts harnessing strange forces to make magic. And sure, anyone could do it, fry an egg, flip a pancake, but the masters did it with style and panache. Greek Benny was no different. Like watching an orchestra conductor lead a symphony, except he wielded a spatula instead of a baton.

"Fitch. Hey. Take a picture it'd last longer."

I looked up. Greek Benny, cigarette hanging out the side of his mouth, t-shirt sleeves rolled up, gave me that stare.

"Sorry, Benny, daydreamin' again."

"And it's payin' off. Must be why you're so successful. Any of this even yours?"

"No," I said. "Just watching an artist at work."

"You want two eggs scrambled, hashbrowns and a short

stack on the side, you come to me. You want art go to a fancy museum."

And that's what made the great ones so great—they didn't know they were great and even if they did they didn't rub it in your face every second. They simply let the ash fall from their cigarette so that it landed in the white of a frying sunny side up egg and then scraped off what they could and covered the rest with a grind of fresh black pepper. Class.

A typical Wednesday in the diner. The usual crew of barflies soaking up the booze with grease, high school brats playing hooky and drinking milkshakes and me, drinking java at the counter. Glenda called it my office, ever since I'd given up the lease on my real one. And about the same amount of people visited me there, round about zero, so I felt right at home. Glenda warmed up my coffee with a splash of the new batch.

"Any case right now, Fitch?"

"Nothing new. Still working on the disappearance of Mr. Jangles."

"A missing person case, huh? Well, look at you."

"He's in fine form this morning," I said, nodding towards Benny.

"He always takes it hard when Li'l Abner gets in trouble."

"Right, Benny and his treasured funnies. It went cold, by the way."

"Huh?"

"The case. Disappeared a month ago and not a trace since."

Glenda shook her head. "That's terrible. His family must be so worried."

"It's been tough on them. The kid, especially."

"And no leads, huh?"

"That briefcase I left here a few weeks ago still around?"

Glenda looked underneath the counter. She pulled out the battered briefcase with the broken lock and the car tire marks. The present I'd given myself following my release from the hospital after the Dead Clown affair had seen better days. I sorted through the collection of paper scraps and receipts inside. "It's not much warmer than that plate of toast that's been sitting on the pass through for the last hour but here's what I got. According to a neighbour, the man seen leaving the scene, and likely the last person to see Mr. Jangles alive, was 'short and squat with a flat face and one hell of a toothy smile'"

Glenda peered inside the briefcase. "That's it?"

"That's it."

"And you didn't crack the case right then?"

"I know, hopeless."

Glenda frowned at the briefcase contents. "So that's your filing system, huh?"

"It looks chaotic but I can find anything at the drop of a hat. Try me."

Glenda grinned, up for the challenge. "Okay, who're you updating on the disappearance?"

"Billy."

"Billy's number, then."

"Easy peasy," I said, closing my eyes. Showing off. I did a little "ta da!" as I showed Glenda the scrap, this time a corner of a napkin.

Glenda was impressed. She took the napkin. Then she wasn't so impressed anymore. "That's the number for the phone on my floor. And I don't remember giving this to you, Fitch."

"Uh…" I said, brain really letting me down.

"We've been getting a lot of strange calls on that phone, in the middle of the night. And no one there. Only some heavy breathing."

"Oh, ah…"

"It's got some of the other girls really spooked. We might call the cops."

"Well…"

Glenda gave me a wink and a finger pistol fire. "I'm messin' with ya, Fitch."

The flop sweat cooled in my armpits. "Right, yeah."

"I mean, we have been getting strange calls but I know you wouldn't do that kind of thing." She was right, it wasn't me, but still not good to be under the microscope lens for fear of a terminal diagnosis. Glenda handed me the napkin scrap. "But back to the case: you tried, that's the important thing, right, Fitch?" Glenda smiled. Her smiles were medicine. Restorative. Lead a man to riches or ruins, but no matter what he'd pick a direction and take it. Straight to the bank or over the side of a cliff, smiling as he went.

"Right," I said.

The door chimes jingled. Glenda went to take the new arrival's order.

"Right," I said again, to myself. And I was even less sure about it this time around. I had tried, but it wasn't even my case, officially. I hadn't been hired, in the true sense of the word. More volunteer, pro bono kind of work. In the months following my near-death-by-circus-elephant I'd ditched the office and the detective act, mostly working for Taffy Pook, hiding in the bushes and behind parked cars, snapping candid shots of insurance fraudsters. But the itch had to be scratched. I needed the juice, the action. I'd never felt more alive than during the search for Jim Baxter's killer and the money he stole from the Dead Clowns. Now, as it turned out, he'd drowned in that lake from crashing his car while drunk and the money had been taken long before I got involved by the building manager, Cleveland Moyer, but still.

And maybe I had no business taking another case, even if it was pro bono. Or maybe it was better than nothing. No one else seemed to care. Regardless, checking in with the family was the right thing to do.

I put a dime in the payphone down the diner hallway and dialed the number from the other paper scrap I dug out of the briefcase. Billy's mom answered. I asked for Billy. She said he was in the kitchen eating a "pee-bee and jay." I read from the script I'd been given and said it was about the math homework. She sounded suspicious like probably I was too old to be calling her son about math homework but she didn't want to be the one to rag on the slow kid who got held back a few years so she said she'd get him.

"Yeah?"

"Billy, it's Fitch."

"Who?"

"Carnegie Fitch. I'm looking for Mr. Jangles."

"Oh. Right. Hold on a sec, will ya?" I heard him mutter to his mom, probably with his hand over the phone. "Okay, I'm back."

"Just checking in."

"I didn't think you'd still be lookin'. I put up those flyers weeks ago."

"You never know when a case can break wide open."

"It's that—"

"I have some good leads."

"Fitch, I hate to break it to you, but I don't think he's coming back."

"Mr. Jangles?"

"No, I don't think so."

"Billy, no."

"Yes, Fitch, he's gone."

"Oh, Billy, I'm sorry."

"I think you should stop calling. My mom gets nosy after every time you call and she's got enough to worry about what with her boyfriend creepin' out in the middle of the night on us. And now I actually have to do my math homework, so thanks for nothin'."

"I'll keep looking, Billy, I promise."

"For Christ sakes, Fitch, it's only a cat. I gotta go. Don't call anymore, okay? Bye."

Well, Billy may have given up but I wasn't about to. It's just a code us non-detectives-working-pro-bono-on-cases-that-aren't-really-cases have. Plus, the picture Billy used on the "missing" posters he stapled on every tree in the area haunted me. They looked so happy together, best friends. Boy and calico cat.

Still, I felt a little bad about misleading Glenda as to the true nature of the "missing person case" so I tried to be the feline and sneak out of the diner. But she saw me heading for the door.

"Go get 'em, Fitch," she said.

3

THREE A.M., the phone in the hallway rang. The sound cut through the heavy silence like a chainsaw through an old tree. I popped my head up off the pillow, listening. Like stepping to the imaginary casino table and rolling the dice. One ring. Come on, two, give me a two. The phone rang again. Come on, three, give me a three. The phone rang again. I waited. No more rings. Jackpot. Snake-eyes, craps, double-sixes, pick your poison.

I rolled out of bed, preened in front of the mirror for a moment. Lick of the hand, smooth of the bed hair. The result not perfect but casually messy. Then a swig of mouthwash and spit it out in the sink. Last, I unlocked my front door, flicked on the bedside lamp and got back in bed.

Ten minutes later, the door opened and there she was: Adora Carmichael. She didn't speak. She dropped her coat where she stood, stepped out of her dress, undid all sorts of complicated latches and clips and an eternity later slid into bed beside me. She was soft in all the right places. Hard where it counted, the head. The gut. We never spoke before.

No need.

We did what man and woman had done since time began and we did it pretty good, all things considered. But we both sensed it wasn't the night to strive for a place in the record books.

After, she lit a cigarette. I fretted about the ash falling on the bed and got up to get her a coffee mug from the sink. She whistled. I blushed. It was in the script and gave us a few minutes to collect our thoughts. Once I'd settled, she put her head on my chest and parked the mug on my stomach. I breathed. She smoked. We did that for a few minutes.

"So how's the supper club business?" I asked.

"The club part I understand. Supper's the tricky part."

"How so?"

"Well, it seems people see 'supper' on a sign and they expect to eat."

"The nerve."

"And they want to eat what's on the menu and have it come out quickly."

"Who are these people, they're ridiculous."

"And so is my kitchen staff. A bunch of hotheads who all think they know best. There was a fight back there last week. Head chef nearly lost a thumb. I fired the whole bunch, brought in a new crew. But they're still learning the ropes. How's business for you?"

"Steady. Taffy's been keeping me if not busy then at least occupied. Still can't find that damn cat, though."

"Nothing else going on?"

"Not really. Should there be?"

She wanted to say something but stopped. I didn't follow up. Then Adora asked if I knew anything about the Disciples of the Sacred Glow. "Some new kooky religion with a preacher-type stirring up a ruckus," she said. "Him and his followers meet out of a warehouse on Water Street, around Cambie."

My neck of the woods for sure. But no, I hadn't heard of them and told her the same. "Any particular reason?"

"Not really. Some things I'm hearing. Keep an eye out, okay?"

"Sure thing." I looked at the mink coat on the floor, the fancy dress in a pile. "Big night at the bowling alley? Did Fran finally get that 300?"

"Funny. No, a fundraiser. New mayoral candidate. He wants to loosen up the liquor laws."

"Adora Carmichael, woman about town. From the circus to the ballot box."

"Carnegie Fitch, man about nothing. From the ditch to the diner."

"Adora Carmichael, looks like a million bucks, swears like a sailor."

"Carnegie Fitch, looks gift horses in the mouth."

"Adora Car—" Once again, her aim was true and I was the bulls-eye. "The tow truck you gave me last summer that I didn't ask for, you mean?"

"I mean."

"Here's the thing."

"This ought to be good."

"I do appreciate the sentiment."

"But?"

"But it would take a lot of work."

"God forbid."

"And I'd have to do it every day."

"You're breaking my heart."

"Well, it's a sad story."

"You got that right. So, better to snap photos from behind bushes, sniff the trail of missing family pets and pine after ditzy diner waitresses, is that it?"

"He's a sweet kid and I'm a sucker for a calico, what can I say? No luck today, though. Hit up a few more shelters but no dice."

"The great mystery deepens. My bet would be on car or coyote. Something got him."

"Could be. I was hoping it wouldn't come to that. You know, for the kid's sake."

"Right, sure. The kid."

"Hey, and Glenda's plenty smart."

"So, make a move then."

"That's just it. Plenty smart."

"What's that say about me, then? Here, now."

"Oh, you're smarter, no doubt, but you're also equal parts damaged and vicious. Kind of evened things out."

Adora ashed out in the mug on my stomach, winked at me and said I sure was a sweet talker for such a sour loner. I said she was pretty sweet herself sometimes when she wasn't so salty. Then we were silent for a few moments. When that was done, she stubbed out the cigarette, moved the mug onto the bedside table and resettled her head in the crook of my arm. And we slept.

4

I WOULDN'T SAY IT WAS A SPRING in my step the morning after Adora's visit but the air up there smelled darn fresh and the sidewalk curbs didn't seem as high, that's for sure. And where did all the chirping birds come from? And though it was unnecessary that they follow me all the way from home to the diner, serenading me with every step, it sure was much appreciated. So much so that I decided to extend my morning stroll a little and see what I could see in that area of Gastown Adora told me about last night.

First up, though, was the Carnegie Library at the corner of Main and Hastings. The library and I, we shared history and a name. Story went, my mother and father met there. According to my mother, my father was an illiterate hound who was only there to sniff crotches. According to my father, well, he decided it would be up to my mother to do all the talking. Barely knew the man, except to know he was a rolling stone who'd been very allergic to moss. Oh well. Some stories are better left untold. All history can't be wrapped up in pretty paper and tied up with a fancy bow.

Next up was a walk down Main to Alexander, where I turned left and went a few blocks, passing the statue of Gassy Jack Deighton, where Water Street sliced west. A few more blocks, past where Cambie Street dead-ended at the railroad tracks, and I couldn't hear the birds what for the hum of the milling crowd. There was a bit of hubbub on the sidewalk outside a warehouse that I didn't remember seeing a hubbub outside before. This was warehouse row and usually the domain of vans and trucks and sour-faced working men with sweat-lined brows and four o'clock scowls waiting for the bell to strike five. The faded sign above the door read BRASHER INDUSTRIES but the freshly painted sandwich board on the sidewalk read THE DISCIPLES OF THE SACRED GLOW WELCOME YOU! and NEW SMILE NEW MAN!

The lineup was a skid row hall of fame. Two Teeth, No Teeth, both English Joes, only one of which was actually English, Short Dog Bob and T-bird Tony, to name only a few. I skipped the line and stuck my head inside to see what was what. At the end of the lineup of human fault and failure was a table with row after row of small white cups lined up, each containing a measure of liquid. A nurse with a starched white uniform, a blue-stripe cap and a very prim-and-proper manner handed one cup each to the men in line and then ushered them towards a Fedora-sporting bulldog in a snappy, tailored three-piece suit. There are times when a man looks more like a dog than seems humanly possible. Short, squat and flat-nosed. And hands like hams that gently led the scuffling, shuffling herd of skid row denizens one-by-one and pointed them to a chair. It all seemed very kind and generous and affable until one poor guy didn't want to sit down after getting his cup of "medicine" and tried to make for the door. Then the bulldog showed why he was there and put a meaty paw on the guy's shoulder and squeezed hard, making sure he found a seat quick and stayed in it, even taking the time out of his busy schedule to crouch down and growl quietly in the guy's ear. What a nice doggie.

"Hey, buddy, you in line or what?"

"Not my kind of elixir, friend."

"Well, whoopety-do for you. Step aside then, why don't ya?"

I stepped aside and instead of backing out the door like I probably should have, like rare ol' Smart Fitch, I did good ol' Dumb Fitch and made my way to the back of the room, near the windows facing the street, grabbing an empty seat at the end of the aisle. I sat down fast before the bulldog could see me. Call me paranoid but I had the idea that I'd gone against company policy by not lining up for the magical elixir and I didn't really want to learn what this company considered appropriate punishment.

The eight rows of folding chairs faced a makeshift stage where, judging by the lights and manufactured pomp and circumstance, a show was about to begin. Climbing up the steps, emerging from the shadows beside the stage, was a man in a bright white suit, carrying a cane. Completing the look was a well-coiffed mane of white hair and a set of teeth that matched the suit. Watts cranked out of his smile like a deranged monkey was manning the facial control switches.

This was trust. This was faith. This was Father. This was the very picture of a learned gentleman who only had your best interest at heart.

"Gentleman, it is a good morning to be alive," he said, a tinge of fire-and-brimstone preacher to his voice. "But to you I say it could be a great morning. As some of you may know my name is Quincy Quest and I'm here to tell you about the wonderful world of sobriety and everything it has to offer.

About family, about togetherness. About what a new smile can do for you, how it can open doors and set you free. Why, I look around me and see a generation of men lost, a generation of men stumbling through the dark. Well, let me show you the way out, towards the light. Join me and I'll introduce you to 'the glow' and its miraculous powers of healing."

As he spoke, the nurse rolled a cart around, handing out more "medication." The bulldog followed. Seeing me empty handed, she offered me the white paper cup. I didn't want to be impolite, or at the other end of a Bulldog's bite, so I accepted. On rolled the cart. On lurked the bulldog.

And on went Quest. And on. Quest spun words like a spider spun silk to catch bugs in its web: on the fly and out of its ass. He was well practiced and must've had some Old West snake oil salesman in his blood. Until the words lost meaning but because they so pleasantly rolled off the tongue and travelled in mesmerizing little swirls and dipsy-dos on the way to the audience's ears that they found themselves nodding and agreeing even though there was a good chance they didn't know what they were nodding and agreeing to. A contract was being written here that they'd inevitably sign though they'd likely walk away not knowing what they were on the hook for or why they'd signed on the dotted line in the first place.

Not that I was completely the one clever sheep among the dimwitted flock. Without knowing what I knew I'm sure the spell would've been more successfully cast. But see, I'd realized a few minutes into the performance that a "performance" was exactly what it was. That under all that hair and makeup, under the pomp and circumstance, was the defrocked dentist of Halifax. The ol' wild card, my campsite nemesis, Copernicus Janssen. The paranoid loon slipping mickeys into his "friends'" coffee for kicks. I'd been on the receiving end of a jolt once-upon-a-time and people said I was around the campfire that weekend but damned if I can remember.

He that had the way with words a snake charmer had with a poisonous viper, bending, curling them to his own ends.

He that was always your best friend, hands on your shoulders, pat, massage, so glad to see you, how *have* you been?

He of the stolen 40 nickels.

I couldn't help myself.

"Boo," I said. Not loud, but not particularly quiet either. I said it again but added a little extra zest. "Boo, Janssen, boo." Jansen stopped and looked towards me, at the back of the room. He leaned down and whispered into the bulldog's ear. Heads turned. I played innocent. I played, "Who said that?" The gentleman next to me was wise. I offered my paper cup as a bribe. He nodded and turned back to the stage, swigging that liquid down. Then he turned back to me. I shrugged "no more." He shook his head, not meaning my serving of "juice." He looked scared. He indicated to my right.

And it wasn't the way I would've chosen to leave the warehouse, in fact I didn't even realize the big front windows out onto the street opened at all. But at least the bulldog was nice enough to open one a crack before shoving me through. I felt like a calf being born in a farmyard, only dropping to Gastown pavement instead of soft grass. And how nice of the bulldog to go around, exiting through the real door, to greet me on the other side. He even helped me to stand. What a gentle doggie.

"Mr. Quest sends his regards," growled the bulldog.

"Well, that's—" The large paw in my belly took the words and the wind right out of me. I decided to sit back down on the street. Better that way. Much nicer. Standing was overrated. I leaned back against the warehouse so my head was level with his paw as he opened it up. And there, as if it always had been, like it'd just popped by to say hello, was a roll of nickels.

The damn 40 nickels.

5

THE OLD LADY, she smelled like lilacs. Dead ones. But expensive. And while they were alive they were undoubtedly cut by the sharpest scissors, housed in the finest crystal vases and sprayed with only the purest of waters. I didn't see her enter the diner but there she was, sitting down across from me in my usual back booth, where, after being accosted by Janssen/Quest's ugly bulldog I'd decided to play a kind of dog myself and lope back and lick my wounds amongst the scritch and scratch of forks and knives against diner plates, the low roar of the lunch crowd, Greek Benny's "Order up!" and the "ding ding" of the bell. That music to my ears, that balm for the soul. Still, it did very little to dull the roar of my gut ache and my dinged-up pride.

The old lady, she didn't say anything right away. She seemed content to silently judge me while removing her white gloves and hat and placing those rare, precious items on the diner table on a handkerchief that I assume she packed in her purse for exactly such an occasion. The trouble with regular folk was we were dirty and had germs. Best to be prepared.

I opened with "Your driver miss a turn somewhere?" and it seemed to barely register, except maybe a little flicker behind the eyes.

"I don't believe he did. You walk very slowly, Mr...?"

"Ah, she speaks. Fitch."

"Fitch, yes, it would be a moniker like that."

"I could change it for you, the price is right."

"That will not be necessary."

"Too bad. There's this silver spoon I've been saving up for. Thought I could do some hobnobbin' with the hoity-toity crowd."

"Silver is very out these days, Mr. Fitch. Might I suggest diamond or platinum?" A faint smile curled her top lip. Touché.

"And you were following me why?"

"Because you were at that meeting this morning but you did not seem interested. I knew for sure when you were accosted on the street."

"Oh, you saw that, did you?" Damn, there went my chance to play tough guy.

"I did."

"All part of the plan."

"It was your intention to get pushed out of a window and beat up in broad daylight?"

"I work in mysterious ways."

She considered this. "So...you were working?"

"Call it more an idle curiosity at this point."

"But you know the man on the stage, do you not?"

"I do, unfortunately. But how do you know that?"

She leaned forward, whispering, "I have a molar inside."

I leaned forward, too. "Really, I have a few myself. Do you mean a 'mole'?"

She sat back, chastised. "You will have to excuse me, Mr.

Fitch, I am rather new to these sordid underworld dealings and the vocabulary that accompanies them."

"Mrs…?"

"Brasher. Kathleen Brasher."

"Like 'Brasher' as in 'Brasher Industries'?" She nodded. I said, "Nice view of Water Street out your warehouse window, but I'm not crazy about the drop." Her eyes clouded over. Rainy season, tears in the forecast. I'd struck a nerve. Now to find out why. "Well, Mrs. Brasher, you followed me for a reason, so why don't you tell me what that reason is."

So, she did, in stops and starts and non-sequiturs, but the gist was that she was the widow of Peter Brasher, who'd died eight months ago in a roofing accident at their Shaughnessy home. Always one for DIY improvement he'd been replacing a few missing shingles when he slipped and fell. Her son, Hugo, former vice president, was now running the family business. And it'd been business-as-usual up until a few months ago, when all of sudden, unbeknownst to her, he shuttered the family business and sold all the equipment.

Glenda walked by. I asked for a glass of water for Mrs. Brasher. Glenda gave me an "everything okay?" side-eye as she poured and I nodded. Mrs. Brasher sipped at the water. Glenda put a comforting hand on her shoulder.

"Ma'am, it'll be okay, whatever the problem is. Fitch is good people. Why, he's working a missing person case pro bono as we speak just because he likes to help."

This perked Mrs. Brasher up. "You are a private detective?"

"I dabble. Mostly insurance fraud cases. I'm the guy in the bushes with the camera."

She put her hand to her throat. "And I am sure I would not know anything about that."

"I'm sure not," I said, not because I figured the Brasher name was squeaky clean by any stretch but living that high up above the ground and you weren't likely to hear the ants move beneath you.

"But you take cases? I could pay you."

This was sticky. I wasn't legally a shamus. No P.I. license in my wallet. True, I craved the action like a bee did the flower, but some cravings might be best left unfulfilled. The last time I'd taken a case, I'd ended up in the hospital after getting repeatedly menaced by asshole clowns, tortured and shot at by a deranged janitor and nearly trampled to death by a stampeding elephant which my client, Adora Carmichael, was riding at the time. Messy like a two year-old eating ice cream. With writing like that on the wall even a blind man would stick his hand out to stop me and say, "You may want to think about this."

Glenda couldn't believe I was hesitating. Mrs. Brasher was clearly a walking neon dollar sign and who couldn't use some of that light in their life. I shook my head and politely-as-possible shooed her away. Best to figure out a little more about this potential "case" before making any decision.

I asked Mrs. Brasher to tell me more about her son's change of heart. "This must've been quite the shock," I said. "But maybe it was a sound business decision. Maybe he knew something you didn't?"

"It is true, I did not meddle in the day-to-day business activities of my husband and I was not about to start with my Hugo. But business was very good and it is all my son has ever known. Perhaps I should have paid more attention after Peter died. Hugo was never the strongest willed of children, despite my husband's efforts to make a man out of him." She sighed. "That is the problem with the children of wealth, I have found. They get everything handed to them and do not know what it is like to be hungry."

"How has your son been lately?"

"I have no earthly idea, Mr. Fitch. I have been living in England with my sister since the accident. Too many memories here. All I know is that since returning, he will not answer the phone or come to the door. He dismissed all the house staff and his driver. There are lights on but the curtains are always closed. I am worried he might be ill."

"And now this preacher character is having his revival meetings at your warehouse, dishing out mysterious medicine and recruiting the locals."

"Yes. And I was hoping you would be able to tell me more about Quest. My 'mole' said you called him by another name before you were accosted."

"Yeah, he went by the handle 'Copernicus Janssen' a few years ago when our paths crossed. And I don't know what he's got going on here, but dollars to donuts it's a scam. Whatever he's calling himself, he's bad news. But I'm beginning to think this is a matter for the police, Mrs. Brasher. If you feel there's been some criminal hijinks."

I got the first smile out of Mrs. Brasher, but it was a pursed one, like sucking on a lemon. She knew something I didn't and was itching to tell me.

"Yes, that is what I thought, Mr. Fitch, so I already went to the police."

"Okay."

"And the detective I talked to nodded with much interest and took notes and got my name and number and said everything he was supposed to say."

"Which was?"

"That he would follow up."

"Sounds promising."

"Well, that was a month ago."

"And still no word from Detective…?"

"Montrose. No, nothing. And I got tired of waiting, so

yesterday I went back to the police station and found out the detective I talked to quit without warning only a few days after I met with him. The other policemen I talked to were nice about it but you could see they did not think there was anything to my story. They did the equivalent of giving a five year-old who cannot sleep a warm glass of milk and a pat on the rear by walking me to the door and telling me Detective Montrose's caseload was being divided up and they would be sure and contact me if they found out anything more about my son."

I sat back. Sure, the ol' dismissive-walk-and-talk. Handshake and a comforting nod, no intention of following up. And detectives quit the force, it happened. Retired, moved away, went into the private security business. There were a lot of reasons to be the cow and head for greener pastures. "So you never saw him again?"

"But I did and therein lies the problem."

"I don't get it."

"It was today," she said, her look a menu serving up two options: half a smile for knowing what I didn't and half a grimace for what that meant. She cleared her throat. She took her time. "When I saw him push you out a window and punch you in the stomach."

I sighed. Oh, that.

6

HALF AN HOUR AFTER Mrs. Brasher left, I dialed the number from the diner payphone. I felt different, more alive. The buzz, the jolt, of having a case, even though I wasn't officially involved. I'd taken down the number where she was staying, the Sylvia Hotel, and promised to take a look into the matter, though I'd warned Mrs. Brasher I wasn't in the business of "business," like giving official reports and receipts and she laughed so much she started to tear up and had to dab at the corner of her eyes with a handkerchief. Of course, not the same handkerchief she used to keep her belongings clean from the diner scourge, no, that would be silly. Her purse must've been stocked with them, one for every occasion. With this handkerchief, a brilliant white one with lace edges, she wiped up the laugh tears, saying she never thought I would be much of a "business" and that's exactly why she wanted to hire me. She'd tried the proper channels and it wasn't working.

The two 20 dollar bills she handed to me like a rookie nurse offered a cloth to a leper sold me on the proposition.

And, she said, if it led to an "investigation" I could "bill" her later. She made it clear, she was a baker: plenty of dough. Pockets so deep there was magma at the end of them. And, of course, there'd be a hefty bonus for getting her son, Hugo, out of the house.

Staring at the twenties in my hand, so crisp and so pretty, I protested enough to feel right about it, almost figuring it'd be rude not to take the advance. Why poor ol' Mrs. Brasher had been forced to come downtown and rub elbows with the vagrants and ruffians and I almost felt bad for her, the poor dear.

Though I wasn't sure whether to be offended or complimented that she hadn't sized me up for having a professional setup. What could I say, I walked what I talked, my advertising equaled my reality. I decided to be neither but to take her money and do my best to see what was going on with her son. Something seemed off. She'd lost a husband to the grave and a son to a castle. Not to mention that Copernicus Janssen was involved and that bastard had his bulldog punch me in the stomach with a roll of nickels. My nickels, to be exact. Well, really, Wendell, the Miner of the Sudbury Basin's nickels but I'd been one to do the dirty work to relieve him of them so I felt a sense of ownership, justified or not.

First things first, I made a call to Adora since it was her tip that got me to the warehouse. I needed to know more about why she wanted the skinny on Janssen/Quest and also ask if she could look into a few things for me. Adora's number was for a service. She never answered direct. I left a message and that was that. Nothing to do but wait.

I went back to my booth and ordered a clubhouse sandwich. Ah, the clubhouse. Why do anything with two slices of bread when you could do it with three? One of mankind's greatest creations, you asked me. And Greek Benny made a pretty good one, with just the right amount of mayo, crisp bacon, thin-sliced tomatoes, lettuce and enough layered turkey to last me to next Thanksgiving.

"Coffee to go with that, Fitch?" asked Glenda, as she set the sandwich down.

"Please," I said. Glenda flipped the mug that was face-down on the table and poured. "I'm goin' easy on the booze but a guy's got to hold on to something, right? Would you date a man with no vices?" I think it came off as conversational repartee but, hey, a little research never hurt.

Glenda smiled. "Only if his biggest habit turned out to be me."

It was a hell of an answer and I had no follow up. But none was needed. The diner was lunch rush busy and Glenda was table-hopping, a consummate pro. I knew it wasn't her dream occupation but she took pride in her job. And so did I, making short work of the clubhouse and the mug of coffee and by the time I'd finished I heard the hallway phone ring and Greek Benny saying, "Fitch, you got a call."

"You rang?" said Adora. Fastest return call ever. Leading with "news about Quest" worked like gangbusters. Now I wanted to know why.

"I did," I said. "Yeah, that Quest thing was a bust. Nothin' there. Bubkus."

Adora paused. "You called to tell me nothing."

"But nothing is something."

"You sure? I heard there were meetings taking place there for sure."

It smelled fishy, a setup. Couldn't put my finger on it exactly but it felt a little like the last time Adora asked me to look into something, when she'd waltzed into my office in a knockout dress and hired me to investigate the death of Jim Baxter, back when she was the Circus Owner and I was the

Pretend Private Eye. She made out to be the grieving "niece," since Jim had been like an uncle and golly gee whiz she was so sure he didn't drink and drive and drown in a lake. But he did. And he also came back to Vancouver to collect the stolen loot he'd murdered Adora's father for and then hidden away before being locked up in prison and Adora's real motivation was to see if I'd stumble upon the money by accident. Agendas like layers of an onion, one inside the other inside the other.

"Well," she continued, "okay then."

"So I should stop snooping around?"

"Who said to snoop around?"

"You did. Not in so many words, but…"

"Sure, stop."

"Okay, fine."

"Good."

"Great."

"Fantastic."

"Wonderful."

Another Adora pause. Then: "Okay, spill it."

"What do you mean?"

"I can read your cards like a book, Fitch, even over the telephone. You're holdin'."

Shit, she was good. Or I was a terrible poker player. I preferred option number one. "Fine. Not only was Quest there, but he's actually one Copernicus Janssen, disgraced dentist and an old crazy hobo campfire pal of mine. And let me be clear: by 'disgraced' I mean 'criminal,' by 'crazy' I mean like a 'deranged fox' and by 'pal' I mean the kind you don't turn your back on if he's holding anything even remotely sharp."

"He sounds charming."

"Oh, he is. But be ready for the oiliest of apple butter talk and check your pockets for your valuables when you're done listenin'. Okay, your turn: why so curious?"

"Like I said, my kitchen staff, the ones I had to fire, they were talking about him. Like he and this 'glow' could heal all their wounds, answer all their problems. Also, a few months before the health club accident, Rolly told me this Quest fella was making a hard play for his tow truck business. He wanted to buy it outright, lock, stock and barrel. Had some big money behind him. But Rolly wouldn't sell. So Janssen seems like a player and I'm curious to know what I'm up against in case his name pops up again."

"And that's it?"

"That's it."

I wasn't sure but took her answer on faith.

Silly Fitch. Never learned.

• • •

Back in my room, I kicked my feet up and sat back. Lots to think about. The chat with Adora and the one that followed had been very helpful. I'd mentioned that Janssen had an ex-cop lackey and wondered if maybe Adora had a connection that could get me the skinny on him. Turned out she did, a police captain looking to make the leap to city hall and she gave me a number, only I should wait a few minutes so she had a chance to call first and "light the candle." Her words. So likely "light the candle" was Adora-speak for "remind the person that I know something they don't want known and so it'd be best to pick up the phone when ol' Fitch calls."

Adora was dangerous, for sure, but on my side at the moment so that had its advantages. Right before we hung up she brought up my tow truck situation again and wondered if I'd find it helpful if she sent someone around to give me a tutorial, tell me what the tow truck biz was like, how to work the rig, etc. Because it just so happened she had the perfect person in mind. Of course she did. I made with the sigh and the "okay, fine, mother" routine because Adora with the scent in her sniffer was impossible to divert off the trail and she did the "that's a good boy" response and that was that. Have a cup of coffee with a grizzled old tow truck vet, why not? But the way Adora sounded so satisfied with herself got me thinking she'd got one over on me, won a contest I didn't know I was competing in. That's how it usually went, "Life with Adora." I could write a book. It'd be short, but salacious.

After waiting five minutes, figuring that was plenty of time, I dialed the number Adora provided. The police captain answered, sounding impatient and ready to get down to business.

"Yes?"

"Yeah, hi. Adora Carmichael gave me this number."

"I was told to expect your call."

"Thanks for taking it."

"I wasn't really given a choice. But it will clear a marker so the carrot has been dangled appropriately. Guess I'm the mule today, chase chase."

My hunch was right. This had to be about more than Janssen wanting to buy Rolly's business and Adora's kitchen staff falling for his preacher-man routine, if she was willing to burn a blackmail match to help little ol' me see a little bit of light. I explained that a Detective Montrose had quit the force a few months back and that anything he could tell me about it and the detective himself would be most appreciated.

He didn't have to think about it for very long. "Okay, yeah, Butch, I know a little about that," he said. "Up and resigned without any warning to go private. Headin' up some bigwig's security detail these days, from what I heard. Stock options and a company car kind of deal."

"Married?"

"I don't think so but he had a steady, a widow with a son. But that's not going too well."

"Why do you say that?"

"Because she said he split. Packed up and vamoosed. She even came by the precinct to check on him a few weeks ago and the desk sergeant told her he'd quit. It was news to her."

"What kind of detective was he?"

"Never heard he wasn't competent but I didn't get the sense he was particularly motivated. Career man, up until recently. Moved his way up the ladder because that's what you do on a ladder, climb, even if the top ain't so grand when you get there. The department Rugby team will probably miss him most of all."

"He played?"

"Nah, not anymore. He was the coach. But he played pro football. Made the BC Lions squad in '51 or '52 and saw a little action. But he had bad wheels so he retired and joined the force. And that's about all I know, so I'd appreciate you letting our shared acquaintance know I cooperated."

I said I would and he hung up, just like that, no goodbye. Some people's manners. Okay, granted, I was getting juice from an orange that didn't want to be juiced but still a little civility went a long way. Life was a vise. We all got squeezed one way or the other. But I was a man of my word regardless, so I fed the payphone another dime and made a call to Adora's service to say that while there wasn't much info I'd got what I needed from her source.

Back at my booth, Glenda swung by to see if I wanted anything and I said no I was fine, I had a glass of orange juice to think about. She glanced down at the tabletop. She looked back to me. No orange juice. She shrugged her shoulders, funny ol' Fitch, and moved on.

So, Janssen's doggie used to play football and had a pair of bad knees now. What a shame, poor pooch. But I still felt the sock in the gut and the rude, rather forced exit through the warehouse window, so I really hoped those rusty wheels hurt him. A lot.

7

SHAUGHNESSY WAS QUIET. Real quiet. I was parked a few blocks off Granville Street and a few south of 33rd Avenue, several houses down from the Brasher house, trying to see what I could see. What I could hear was barely a sound through the open window of my tow truck. Only the gentle breeze through the leaves, the hum of a distant lawnmower and a bird chirp now and then. Mostly, what you could hear, if you listened closely enough, was the sound of the money making whoopie. Money making money making money. Like a dating service for the almighty dollar and only family oriented money wanted. Single money not ready to mingle need not apply.

And it was a spectator sport around here, no doubt. Not much to do but sit back and watch the money procreate. Not that it was my kind of game but I could imagine that in the mansions on the wide streets under the thick foliage of the tree canopies it was quality entertainment. Not like downtown, Gastown, the warehouse, the docks. There it was hard graft, lift that, put that there, sweat, lunch break, sweat, quittin' time, do it again the next day. Every dollar too tired at night to do much in the way of baby making.

I sat back in the seat and thought about the information pie on the table in front of me. I wanted to eat the whole thing but all I could put on a plate was a small slice. Still, Mrs. Brasher deserved an update so I'd called her prior to setting out for Shaughnessy. She wasn't as impressed as I'd hoped.

"I fear my money may have been ill spent," she said.

"It's only been a day."

"Could the Egyptians have built the pyramids with that attitude, Mr. Fitch?"

It seemed an unfair comparison but she seemed so set on it, I didn't try to push her off. Instead, I said I was going to be snooping around her house later and I'd probably have her son, Hugo, out by teatime so best prepare the scones.

When in doubt, swing for the fence.

Like here, Shaughnessy, where the houses were big, the egos bigger. Take the Brasher mansion, for example. Only a ridiculous confidence, a sense of rabid entitlement, built something like that. A manifest destiny to live like Kings and Queens. Although, the place was only impressive if you liked castles. Otherwise, ho hum, yeah yeah, so what? Parapets and wide, sweeping balconies. All on a corner lot with a driveway, a wrought iron gate to keep the riffraff out and enough grass to make a par five with a dogleg left feel jealous. And a guy could get to thinking they didn't want people snooping around what with the giant hedges bordering the property. The nerve. Made my job trying to see what was inside a hell of a lot harder. No respect for the nosy was what it was.

Though I was about to find out that getting inside the house would be the least of my worries. Because that was when a pair of hands suddenly grabbed me around the collar and yanked me up and out through the open window. I made a whole bunch of sounds not fit for the ears of children and ended up on the grass beside my truck in a heap. With, surprise, surprise, the ex-cop bulldog standing over me.

The doggy growled. "You're makin' this too easy, Fitch."

"I don't see your owner. That's nice that he lets you off the leash sometimes." He raised a paw in a threatening manner. "Okay, okay," I said. "Points for the window being all the way down this time. And for symmetry: we've gone from out to in and in to out. But I didn't know lil' doggies could sneak up like that. You learn that in the force?"

"And did you learn at dick school to show up to a stakeout in a tow truck with your name on it?"

"Okay, you got me there. I'm still workin' out the kinks. But to what do I owe the honour?"

"Mr. Quest, he'd like to see you."

"And if I don't want to see him?"

"It's not really a question."

"I see. Well, then, my answer is…" And then I kicked him in the right knee, hard. If I'd been standing it'd have been like stomping on a bug. But I was horizontal and with all that force going sideways the knee went a direction it wasn't designed to. He screamed. And while he busied himself with that, I got up and ran. And I'd love to say I was the graceful sprinter rounding the corner in the 200m but no track, only sidewalk, and it was a pure panic run. Zero plan, simply get the hell away. I looked back, which was a mistake. Sure, the bulldog was on the ground on his side, clutching his ruined wheel, so no problemo there, but when I turned around again I ran straight into a brick wall.

A wide, squat, brick wall in the middle of the sidewalk.

Strange place for one of those, I thought, as I hit it.

As the wind left me.

As I stared at up at the sky, gasping like a fish.

• • •

I ended up on a plush leather couch in a room with a big desk and a fireplace going gangbusters. Lots of wooden bookshelves lined with impressive tomes against green wallpaper. The brick wall I ran into outside was there, too. And so was Janssen. He had too many teeth. They were real bright. "Ah, yes, there's that colour in your face again. You had us worried, Mr. Fitch."

"Us?" I said, not really pronouncing it properly. My tongue wasn't fully cooperating.

"Yes," said Janssen. "My associate and I. You gave us a scare."

Oh. The brick wall I'd run into was a short wide man in a short wide brown suit with a brown bowler hat to match. And I swear, no neck. He was all big melon and chest and what neck there was looked like you could saw it in half and count the rings. So, easy mistake. But it made more sense now that I knew it was a man, not a brick wall that had put me over his shoulder and carried me into the house like a sack of potatoes. "Sorry for the inconvenience," I said.

"As he is sorry for getting in your way, aren't you, Reynold?" Reynold grunted. Janssen backed up and sat on the corner of the desk, lifting a snifter of brandy to his lips. He took a sip and swallowed. "Sometimes my aides don't know their own strength and simple requests like asking them to escort a certain old friend inside for a certain discussion can lead to a very different result than expected."

The room was hot. Sweat poured down my face.

"A fire in May?" I said.

"You wouldn't stop shivering."

"I'm allergic to bouncing off brick walls, I guess. Speaking of the unexpected how is your bulldog?"

"If you're referring to Mr. Montrose then he's likely seeking medical attention as we speak."

"The veterinarian, huh? Hope you got a good one. I had a friend once, took his dog in for worm shots and they ended up castrating him. Not the owner, the dog."

Janssen laughed. "Ah, yes, the trademark 'Fitch funny.' It takes me back. Think you can sit up now?"

I sat up. Everything worked. It was a relief. "Reynold's the quiet type, eh?"

"Oh, yes," said Janssen. "Never speaks, actually. Chooses not to, I suppose. But who knows? He doesn't talk. Though my employment of him isn't hinged on his ability to communicate."

"Only with his fists."

"What you must think of me, Mr. Fitch. Like some common goon, I bet."

"Janssen, Janssen."

"Actually, I go by 'Quest' now."

"I heard. That was quite the performance the other day. Because that's what it is, right? You don't believe that nonsense, do you?"

He looked like maybe he was about to give me the business, the show, the pizzazz, but then thought better of it. Instead, he smiled and said, "Every sheep needs a shepherd. And I'd rather be the shepherd. It pays better."

"Well, you and your special medicine sure got the rummies attention."

"Too bad you had to leave halfway through."

"I never was very patient."

"I seem to remember that." Janssen smirked and reached

into his pocket. He put the roll of nickels on the blotter, standing them on one end next to a newspaper folded at the half and open to what looked like the obituaries.

And there they were: my 40 nickels.

I gave him the sweetness. "Janssen you're a real peach. So nice of you to save them for me all this time. But I'll take 'em back now."

"Oh, I don't think so," he said, giving me back the sweetness covered in icing with sprinkles on top. "These nickels have become very special to me. A good luck charm, as it will. Every time I'm in front of an audience I find their presence very comforting." He placed the roll of nickels on a tiny pedestal on the desk, one he seemed to have had made custom so it fit oh-so perfectly. "Why, can you believe, that it was the very day I attained these nickels that I first conceived of the DSG? And I have you to thank for it. You pointed me in the direction of the television medium and I took it the next logical step."

"Logical?"

"Well, profitable."

I looked around. "Seems so. Fancy digs."

"Hugo's a dear friend to the cause and is very supportive."

"Clearly. Say, he's not around, is he?"

"Why, yes he is. Ever since his father passed, Hugo's become quite a homebody." Janssen leaned forward, like we were gossiping and I was getting the primo dirt. "The death was quite hard on him. Happened right outside this window, actually. Fell off the roof, the poor man. Accidents in the home are so tragic. But I digress. Back to the nickels. Let's say you did think you'd been wronged in some way. That I 'stole' your property, despite you having stolen it shortly before." He removed a chequebook from the desk drawer then rang a little silver bell on the desk. A moment later, a man who appeared to be Hugo Brasher or at least his robot look-a-like entered the room and stood at Janssen's side. According to the picture his mother had given me, the likeness was there, but there was no life in his face. Slack features, eyes staring straight ahead. I wondered if Hugo donated some brain cells to the cause, too. I'd seen lobotomy patients with more verve.

"You would accept a cheque, Fitch, would you not?"

I stared at Janssen. My heart pounded. The air got thick. Here was another potential payday, exactly what I'd always been waiting for. The buried treasure, the quick score. Like with the Dead Clown money only that was scooped up by Cleveland Moyer, the manager of the building where Jim Baxter hid it, months before I got on the scene. I never had a shot. But the dream of it still burned bright when I closed my eyes.

"That's some script you're writing there. Usually the payoff comes at the end."

"I like to do things differently, you should know that. And why should I beat around the proverbial bush, when we both know what you want. Now, for the amount." He readied the pen and made exaggerated "this is a man thinking very hard" sounds. "Obviously, the insult is worth more than the measly two dollars the nickels are worth. Mental pain and suffering? How much money would alleviate that?" Janssen tapped his finger and Hugo bent down. He whispered in Hugo's ear and Hugo wrote out a cheque. Then he put the pen down and stood up. "Thank you, Hugo," said Janssen, "that will be all."

Hugo left the way he arrived, dead-eyed and limbs by his side. Janssen ripped the cheque from the book and held it up. I got closer. It was made out to Carnegie Fitch and had four zeros. Boy, I sure liked a zero when it brought friends.

And I couldn't help but dream the ol' dream again. The one with the easy cash and where Glenda taps me on the shoulder and points up at the Eiffel Tower because we're in Paris due to the fact that I'm so rich and sophisticated. Isn't it beautiful? she asks. Yes, I say, yes it is.

Back in reality, I took the cheque from Janssen. "A piece of paper like this creates questions," I said. "Namely what do I have to do for it?"

"Nothing more than what you're doing now," he said. "Simply walk that cheque to the bank, deposit it and enjoy the results."

"No strings?"

"Only if you consider silence a string."

"So that's how you got to your bulldog, too, huh? I heard he left the force so fast you could see the dust trail he left in his wake."

"No, I simply mentioned that I had a job opening for a Vice President of Security and mentioned the yearly salary. City policeman do not make much money. A shame, really." Janssen shook his head. Mock sadness.

And I'd never really noticed before, probably because in our hobo campfire days we all had that scrawny, down-and-out look, but with steady meals and a regular dose of soap Janssen cleaned up pretty well. With a mug like his, all ruddy-cheeked and eye-gleam, he probably could've been in the pictures. Maybe not the starring role but definitely side-kick material. Though I wasn't sure the big screen would've been wide enough to fully capture the sheer size of his huge, ego-inflated head. And those teeth, yikes. Probably flash-fry the film and blind the leading lady.

"That the same hex spell you bewitched Hugo with?"

"Hardly black magic, my dear Fitch. The poor boy was distraught after the sudden death of his father and simply needed a shoulder to cry on."

"Oh, right. So his pops, Brasher, the elder, slipped did he?

An accident in the home? I wonder about that. You're like someone else I know. Always lots of accidents, especially tragic ones, happening around them…but always to other people."

"Oh, Mr. Fitch, I'm unlike anybody you know, I promise you."

"You are a special kind of crazy, I'll grant you that."

His brow furrowed. He got cross. "Oh, now don't use the 'c' word, we don't like that kind of thing."

We? I thought. Interesting. I decided not to follow up. More like a dusty gold nugget to put in the pocket and polish up to reveal at a later, more opportune date.

"And that's the thing with a hypothesis, Fitch. One can never really know for sure."

"True," I said. "Just like one can never really know what they'll do in a certain situation. Like this one, for example. I've dreamed of being handed something like this all my life. In fact, last year I thought I was getting close. But alas, no cigar. And now here it is. And here I am. And I'm doing this." I folded the cheque several times and ripped it into pieces. The pieces fluttered to the floor like confetti. Very expensive confetti.

Janssen shrugged. So be it. "That tells me that you're more stupid than I'd even imagined, Fitch. I wouldn't think a man in your situation would play so fast and loose with a cheque like that."

"And what situation would that be, pray tell."

"Well, let's see. Perpetually broke and no prospects, for starters. Yes, while I'm sure you've spent the last few days lifting my rocks I've been lifting yours. Why I found out you don't have an investigator's license or a tow truck license. Imagine that. You're a little child in an adult's world. Always playing games and angles. Still nothing, Fitch, a nobody. Just like when I left you in Toronto."

"Hey, that's not fair. I have a hot plate now."

Janssen chuckled. "Well, I stand corrected. You've come a long way. Congratulations, you can heat up canned soup in your fleabag flophouse apartment."

"Hey, again, that's a shot below the belt. It's a cockroach infestation not fleas."

"Always the joker. And to think I thought you might be an asset to the team and, at the very least, a silent partner. I guess there's only one more thing that might change your mind."

"Oh yeah, what's that?"

"Do you want to see it, Fitch?"

"It?"

"The glow."

"Do I want to see the glow?"

"It's a simple question."

I thought about that. "It's really not."

"I think you should. A man like you could learn a lot from it."

"A man like me."

"Yes."

"Could learn a lot from…?"

"The glow."

"Right, the glow."

"Yes, exactly."

"Is it you flashing them pearly whites in a dark room?"

"No, sorry to disappoint."

"Hmm. Okay, so what's 'the glow'?"

"It might be easier if I show you."

"Why don't you give me a hint? I have a bad heart."

"I really think I should show you."

"And I really think I'm fine not to see it." Which I

absolutely was but Reynold grunted and in that caveman-esque sound, one forged on the open plain, in fire and ice, I heard the sound of snapped bones and screaming. I understood my options. "Okay," I said, "sure."

Janssen winked at me, pleased as punch. "Excellent."

So, I guess I was going to see the glow.

8

WE TOOK HUGO'S CAR, a cherry Lincoln Continental, although the way Janssen acted as if it was his, it was easy to tell the vehicle was yet another appropriation for the "cause." Driving was a goon I hadn't been unfortunate enough to meet yet and he had an air of recently-washed about him. I may have seen him around Gastown, wearing out a bar top with his elbows at noon, but maybe not. Whoever he was, whatever back alley doorway he recently stumbled out of, he now had a nice suit and a nice hat and a nice new set of slightly-oversized teeth and he drove sure and steady. Like Reynold he didn't say much but I suppose he hadn't been hired for his conversation either. Janssen rode shotgun. In the backseat it was Reynold behind Janssen and me on the driver's side. I stared out the window, feeling Reynold's gaze bore a hole into the side of my skull.

Every stop sign and red light, my hand crept for the door. And Reynold would grunt. And I'd understand my options very clearly, once again. We were developing quite the friendship.

Behind us, another Disciple of the Sacred Glow goon

followed in my tow truck, as we went from toney Shaughnessy back to my neck of the woods, downtown. Our destination was, unsurprisingly, the Brasher family warehouse on Water Street. The goon pulled the Continental in behind a beat-up Buick blocking the loading bay doors. My tow rig was nowhere to be seen.

"One of ours, Sir?" asked the driver.

"No," said Janssen, "I don't believe it is. Take care of it, please."

"Right away." The driver hopped out of the car and walked across the street to a phone booth, where he made a quick call. When he got back in the car, he said, "Anytime now, they have someone close."

Janssen nodded. "Excellent."

So, we waited. I had to really fight the urge to break the uncomfortable silence with a wisecrack but something told me now wasn't the time. Reynold was in the punishment business and I didn't want a wisecrack to turn into a skull crack.

After a few minutes, a tow truck pulled up beside the Continental, driver side to driver side. The goon rolled the window down, said, "Hey" and nodded towards the Buick. Then the tow truck driver quickly and methodically spent the next ten minutes hooking up the Buick to his rig and drove it away, but not before standing in the wash of the Continental's headlights and nodding respectfully at Janssen. Janssen gave a quick wave back. And that was that.

"Okay, let's go," said Janssen when the tow truck had turned the corner. He had a key on his ring that opened the loading bay door. Inside, was a wide-open space with boxes of pamphlets, buttons and other paraphernalia. A propaganda drop. "It's from here that we spread the message, Fitch," he said, enjoying the scene.

"This is what you wanted me to see?"

Janssen shook his head. "This is only the beginning. Reynold, show the man to the back."

Reynold put his giant mitt on my neck and led me through the boxes to the rear of the warehouse. Janssen got another key off his ring and opened a trap door in the floor. The door swung up and out on a recessed hinge, revealing a staircase. Janssen tugged on a string attached to a bare bulb and it illuminated the way down. Reynold nudged me in the back. I followed Janssen down the stairs. At the bottom, he wandered off in the half-light and I heard him flick another switch.

"Oh, shit," I said when I got to the last step, realizing I was in a whole heap of trouble. In the middle of the large, open space was a movable overhead light on a stand. And in the spotlight was a single dentist chair. Janssen removed his jacket, hung it on a coat rack next to the dentist setup and rolled up his sleeves.

"Let's take a look in that mouth of yours, shall we, Fitch?" he asked, smug, no disguising the fun he was having.

Reynold's hand kept me moving forward. My feet didn't want to participate but they kept moving. Stupid feet. "I… no…fine," I said, tongue heavy and unwieldy. Sweat popped at my hairline.

Janssen rolled a stainless steel table on wheels beside the chair. On it were pointy things and gougey things and scrapey things and I was getting a bit concerned. "Oh, Fitch, surely a quick look. When was the last time you visited the dentist?"

"Years. And there's a reason for that."

"But that's the problem, Fitch. Rot creeps in. Rot ruins lives. So new smile, new life. Better living through dentistry."

"That sounds familiar."

"Yes, it's a riff on the DuPont slogan, but I don't suppose they'll mind, do you? It's an informal slogan."

"And you know me, Janssen: Mr. Formality. Official slogans only." I hammed it up, going full '50s TV ad, "'Wonderbread: Builds Strong Bodies 8 Ways.' 'Things Go Better With Coke, Drink Coca-Cola.'"

Janssen chuckled. "A man of the times. Bravo. Anything else you'd like to share?"

"Nah, I've got an informal slogan too: always leave an audience wanting more. So I'll just be go—" I turned to leave but Reynold grabbed me by the shoulders. He had one hell of a grip and meant business.

"Sit, Fitch," said Janssen.

I sat. Reynold pushed me back and strapped my arms and legs down. Janssen ratcheted the chair back. "No wonder you got chased out of Halifax," I said. "Your customer service needs a lot of work."

"My 'customers,' as you call them, Fitch, are the happiest former winos and hobos on the block. My work changes lives. The DSG is a family for the lost, the scared. I give them what they so desperately crave, normality. Bring them under my wing. And now, little birdie, I want you under there, too. So open your mouth."

I shook my head. Janssen said that was okay, fine, suited him. He seemed glad I'd made that choice, which meant he had another way in mind. I was pretty sure that way was Reynold cracking my jaw open like it was oyster-shucking time. I opened my mouth.

"Excellent," said Janssen, strapping on a headlamp. "Now, let's get started." He leaned in, the glint of two stainless steel tools in his hands.

I felt the tools enter the private space of my mouth, caressing gum, clicking slowly and carefully over teeth. One instrument held my tongue aside while the other probed. Janssen took his time. My heart rate spiked. I retched, nearly throwing up.

"Relax, old friend, I'm simply having a look see. And what I see is that I have my work cut out for me."

The words "work" and "cut" didn't calm me down one bit. I had the chair arms in a death grip. I dripped sweat. My heart rate had spiked and stayed there. It was fight or flight but neither was an option. I wondered how it all went wrong and if it'd ever go right again.

Janssen whistled as he inspected and measured, a merry and lilting tune. He was a man in his element, doing what he'd been trained to do. Hands down the single most bizarre experience of my life and I'd been specializing in bizarre lately what with nearly getting run over by a stampeding elephant last summer and tortured by a cash-crazy janitor with a couple of alligator clips, a car battery and a decaying moral center gooey with rot. Life sure was full of surprises. As was Janssen of words. So many words that when he wasn't whistling, he opened his mouth and out they came, one after the other after the other.

He told me that the human body had so many nerve endings in the mouth that the dentist had to be careful, or it really could be quite painful.

He said, "I remember that you used to try to whistle" and I said, "I hay ih uh e euz I its ahen ooen ay om ah uh ahihihn" and he said, "Excuse me?" and removed the tools from my mouth and I said, "I gave it up because my lips wanted union pay from all the practicing" and he laughed and said, "Same ol' Fitch, always a joke" and then shoved the tools back inside.

He told me about leaving me behind at the campsite, years ago, after he'd stolen the roll of nickels. How he'd walked through the neighbourhoods of Toronto that night, creeping in the dark, peeking into windows, seeing the happy, content families in front of the television. Basking in the glow, accepting its warmth. And it was that night that he realized how he could take his passion for helping the poor and forgotten and combine it with this new element of television, of normality. And so, Disciples of the Sacred Glow was born.

He said he was very confident that I was snooping around on behalf of Hugo's mother but what he couldn't figure out was who her mole was, though he was sure there was one, since Mrs. Brasher was about as slick as sandpaper. There had been a number of inductees recently and he was convinced one of them was a spy. But no matter, he said. He'd soon figure it out and he was very much looking forward to a face-to-face meeting.

He said he was done with the examination.

He said he had something to show me because he needed a few moments before the operation began, to prep the correct dentures for my mouth.

He said "New smile, new life."

I didn't get it.

And then I got it and I laughed. I laughed big and I laughed long.

Janssen was going to remove all my teeth.

I was so conflicted. Janssen was a lot of bad words I couldn't remember anymore but he was pretty darn funny, too.

And handsome, I had to admit.

And maybe he was right because new smile, new life. New opportunity. Maybe it was my old crooked teeth holding me back. And for the first time since being in the warehouse basement, I felt…calm. Relaxed. Nothing weighed on me, my bones felt light. Good thing I was strapped in or I might float up to the ceiling. And as long as I listened to Janssen everything would be okay. And it was hunky dory with me that Janssen tipped my chair back up, moved all the dentistry equipment away and then turned off all the lights. Cool as a cucumber, that was me, ol' Fitchy, strapped to a chair and sitting in the dark with evil but handsome people all around, scurrying around in the background like rats. But rats were A-OK. No problemo. Who didn't love a hairy rat? I heard the squeak of wheels approaching and then a large television flicked to life in front of me. Not tuned to any channel, but the sheer bright white of the snow was shocking, mesmerizing. And that's when I realized:

It was the glow.

And my new teeth would be the glow, too.

And the glow was beautiful.

The glow was everything.

The glow truly was blessed.

Janssen began to speak and his voice was everywhere, all around me. In each ear, flowing into every nook and cranny of my brain. And I was getting it. I could see now. The glow. Yes.

The glow was beautiful.

The glow was everything.

The glow was blessed.

The glow was beautiful.

The glow was everything.

The glow was

Gone, suddenly.

Janssen's voice, too.

And there was nothing.

Only the scurrying of rats.

Many rats.

And darkness.

It was the void.
I got scared.
My heart rate spiked.
I screamed.
I screamed again.
I heard a "Hey!" followed by an "Ooh" followed by a loud crash.
Then I felt hands on me, undoing the straps, pulling me along, further into the dark, the un-glow.
Into the void.
The hands pulled.
The void was lit with thin strands of light.
I could see more now.
The hands belonged to a small pale ghost.
The ghost looked back at me and grinned.

And it felt like an end.

But it was a beginning.

9

AND LIKE MOST BEGINNINGS it was a rude awakening.

De-tethered from the glow, I was being ushered to the land of the dead by the small pale ghost to be reborn on the other side, from the void. To then be forced out into the unforgiving un-glow.

My legs were rubber.

I couldn't walk properly, no strength.

The ghost was still there, guiding me farther out of the void.

The ghost yelled.

The ghost pulled.

I realized this ghost did not have my best interests at heart.

So I shoved the ghost away.

I ran.

I bolted on unsteady legs.

There were flashing lights and broken sounds.

I had crossed over.

I was seeing things how they really were.

40 NICKELS

The city morphed, back into a forest. Paved streets became muddy paths. The people changed in front of me, de-evolving as well. Here in the un-glow, on the other side of the void, they could show their true form to me. Their bottom teeth were wicked fangs that curled up over their lips, towards their misshapen noses. They cast off their human wrapping and became goblins loping along the sidewalks. Their skins were a sickly green hue with grody yellow and red splotches.

The temperature dipped. I shivered. The goblins blew clouds of breath from moist nostrils. Bits of stringy meat hung from their lips.

Goblins watched as I passed by, sensing my newly born status, probing my weak-limbed-knock-kneed gait for weak spots, for opportunity. Hunters and I was the hunted.

Like a fawn is a target for the wolf.

And me without a mother deer in sight.

Seeking shelter, I fled into the underbrush.

I stumbled down a steep mud path.

I emerged in an enclosed glade, where only shafts of moonlight lit a group of man-goblins standing in a circle, around a large ornate table, carved of an ancient, dark wood. They spoke in a strange tongue. They played a game of sorts. They used long femur bones to knock painted baby skulls, smoothed and rounded, against each other. The object of the game seemed to be getting the baby skulls into the corners, where they would disappear down the gullet of human skulls, their jaws pried unnaturally open.

I wanted to leave but I didn't know which way to go. Or how to move my legs anymore. I froze. I went fear-stiff.

Good thing I was downwind. They couldn't smell me. Perched on the edge of the light, I decided not moving was the wisest strategy.

And I became fascinated by their guttural grunts and

odd sounds as I watched their game unfold. I wanted to turn away but could not. Their game was one of war, separation, a cleaving. A domination of humanity, bodies becoming tools of entertainment.

Until a goblin turned to me, nodding.

I was wrong.

They'd smelled me all along.

The creature stepped away from the grassy glade, the game, and loped towards me, bulbous lips glistening in the moonlight.

I couldn't move. My limbs were solid blocks.

The goblin grabbed me by the leg and upended me with ease. It dragged me to his lair, where it laid me down into a special sacrificial chair, exposing my tender neck for the bloodletting. It unsheathed a blade from a scabbard around its chest as it spoke ancient incantations in its goblin tongue.

I didn't have any screams left.

So I started laughing and laughing.

The fawn will do that, give up.

Say, "You got me."

Welcome the wolves' fangs to its throat.

Nod hello to Death.

10

I WOKE UP PROPPED up against a log at Kitsilano beach, legs half buried in the cold sand. I could see the tips of a pair of shoes. I wiggled my toes and the shoes moved—good, they were mine.

Small waves lapped against the shore. The tide was coming in. The sky was blue.

I was alive. Sort of.

My head pounded. My tongue was uncooked steak. I had dry, cracked lips and sand in every nook and cranny. And I'd been shit on by a flock of seagulls. Or maybe only one bird. Though, in that case, one with some serious digestion tract issues.

Years ago, must've been late 40s, I'd flipped through a copy of Life magazine I found on the street and inside was a four-page spread on this artist fella, Jackson Pollock, and his style of drip painting. Something about his work always stuck with me. And now I resembled one, a museum piece for the ages:

The Seagull (b. 1953)
Fitch Visits the Beach, 1958
Bird shit on human canvas

Or, look at it another way and I was road kill left for dead, half buried in the sand and dirt and grit at the side of the highway.

"Anyone get the license plate of that truck?" I said, sitting up. The seagull sitting on the next log over didn't answer and neither did anybody else because there was no one else around. "Was it you?" I asked the seagull. Better to be upfront, air out the laundry. I felt like we might be sharing the next few minutes on this planet as the waves came in and the sun rose over the mountains and if the bird did it, okay, we could get past it and be friends. Everything needed to poop and sometimes you were the pooper and sometimes you were the poopee. Life worked like that. Shit and be shit on, the endless cycle.

The gull didn't answer.

"Silent type, huh?"

Guilt ridden, the gull squawked and flew away.

"I forgive you," I yelled, which was silly but it let me know that what happened to me hadn't seemed to have left any permanent damage to the ol' noggin, at least nothing other than the inevitable nightmares I'd be having until I slept the long sleep in the pine box. Yes, I could still make with the talk. And after a few more minutes of collecting myself, I realized I could still make with the walk so I got up and hoofed it over the Burrard bridge towards downtown.

No land speed records were broken that day. Not by me, anyway. There may have been a few records set as various pedestrians hurried around me and past me and generally did their very best to stay away from the limping, smelly weirdo covered in bird excrement. They made with the wide eyes and the shakes of the head and I made with the head down and focus on keeping my feet moving.

When I finally made it back to Gastown, the ghost was waiting patiently for me, sitting on the rear bumper of my tow truck, legs swinging, reading a book. There, just like that. The ghost.

"Hello," I said, voice shaky. Figured it was best to face madness head on at this point.

The ghost waved.

The ghost tipped its head to the side.

Okay, I saw it now. The ghost was, in fact, a teenage girl, maybe 14 years old.

"Hi," she said. Then, "You look like shit, Fitch."

"So nice of you to notice. And I look better than I feel, believe it or not."

"What happened to you the other night? You acted real loony and pushed me away after I got you out of that warehouse. I was trying to help."

"Right, sorry about that. I'm still piecing things together. Been waiting long?"

"Off and on for a few days."

"Days?"

She nodded. "I watched from the doorway across from your building as some guy parked your tow truck and then took off. I was curious so I followed him to the warehouse. Saw you sitting in the Continental while that palooka hooked up the Buick. Then you were forced inside and I decided you needed help. What'd they do to you, anyway?"

"Drugged," I said. I'd gone over it in my head and it was the only thing that made sense.

"By that preacher guy, Quest?"

"I think so. He was about to remove all my teeth and give me a new set of fake choppers. You saved my bacon, no doubt."

"He was gonna remove all your teeth?"

"That's his racket. Gets the down-and-out in the door with some 'medication,' some fancy talk, a promise of 'new smile, new life' and then hands out doses of the crazy juice and gives 'em the business with 'the glow.' After that, a little dental surgery between friends, where he removes every one of their teeth and replaces them with dentures. So they walk away with a new set of choppers, probably convinced he'd helped them."

She frowned. "You okay, Fitch?"

No, not at all. In no way shape or form was I okay. Instead, I said, "Three things. One, what's your name? Two, how did you know to find me at the warehouse? And, three, why did you help?"

She put out her hand. I shook it. She said, "Eleanor Stevens, but call me 'Ellie.' And Adora told me about you. She said you needed help with this here tow rig." Ellie patted the side of the truck. "Learning the business."

"And she sent you?"

Ellie's jaw went out, defiant. "Yeah, what's it to ya?"

"Nothin'," I said, "just not who I expected."

"Because I'm a girl?"

"No, because you should be doin' algebra equations and gossipin' about boys not towing cars and sneaking into warehouses at night to save the likes of me. Though I won't complain about the last one."

"Yeah, well, my dad never wanted to raise me square. And I do go to school but it's Saturday today. And boys are dumb."

"You're making very valid points." Then it dawned on me. "Stevens? As in Rolly Stevens, the tow truck king of Vancouver?"

"The very one."

"I'm sorry about what happened to your father."

She looked down at the ground, didn't answer. I thought back: her father, Rolly, had "slipped" in the shower at his health club and gone into a coma. He'd died a few days later. In my scattershot, throw-as-many-darts-at-the-board-in-hopes-that-one-hits-the-target accusatory rant at Adora, when she visited me in the hospital, after the Dead Clown affair, I'd essentially laid the blame at her feet. And she neither officially denied nor confirmed the accusation. But I'd always assumed it was part of her strategy to take over the Vancouver criminal rackets. But I was second-guessing that now and thrown for a loop, truth be told. Though the loop was about to get even more twisty and dangerous, especially when the bomb dropped and blew the tracks up altogether.

Detonation in five…

"By the way," said Ellie, "neither are you, you know. What I expected. You look like a guy that could make a bum sit up after you walked by and thank the heavens above he's not as low down as you."

Four…

I gave her the fist gun and an index finger trigger pull. "And you've got Adora's aim."

Three…

Ellie blew the smoke off the index finger of her own pistol. "Of course."

Two…

And then I saw it: the jaw line, the nose. "Wait, you mean…?"

One…

Ellie nodded. "Oh, you didn't know? Figures she wouldn't talk about it." She stopped and kicked the tire of my tow truck. "Yeah," she said, looking up at me. "Adora Carmichael is my mom."

Boom.

11

IN THE DINER WASHROOM, I did my best to clean up. What I really needed was a complete overhaul, to be taken apart and itemized, each piece considered for its continued value to the whole. Once the extent of the damage was assessed, broken parts could be fixed or replaced, as necessary. Then, a patient re-build and a nice buff and polish to get the finished Fitch ready for the showroom floor. Instead, I made do with rinsing my hair in the sink, scrubbing my hands and face with all the soap I could get out of the dispenser and throwing my suit jacket into the garbage. It was beyond salvage.

Ellie was waiting in the booth, talking to Glenda. I sat down across from her.

"You sure you're old enough to drink coffee, honey?"

"Very sure."

Glenda looked at me quizzically. "Should she be…?"

I shrugged and nodded sure, why not. None of my business, really. So Glenda poured us both a cup and said she'd be right back with our pie. The pie was Glenda's idea. My stomach was a small boat on high seas, rolling with the waves, unsure whether it would capsize or not.

Ellie Stevens drank her coffee with about a litre of milk and a cup of sugar, turning a fine cup of quality joe into a sugary sweet concoction. She added the ingredients in her dessert recipe and stirred a whirlpool.

"The hard stuff, huh?" I asked.

"Yeah, you gotta problem with that?"

"Nope." I mocked digging in my inside pocket, glancing furtively around. "You want some whisky in there, too?"

Her eyes lit up. "Yeah, okay."

I took my hand out of my pocket, nothing there. Only the middle finger I was giving her. "Yeah, right, you're still a kid."

She sighed and rolled her eyes so far back I worried they wouldn't re-center. "And you're still an asshole."

"Everybody needs one."

"Eww."

Glenda came back with two pieces of cherry pie. Now that the food was in front of me I realized it'd been a long time since I ate. No longer the small boat on the high seas, my stomach was a growling bear nosing through a campsite saying "feed me." I made short work of the pie and sat back, letting the sugar and fat do their work.

After Ellie had dropped the Adora/mom bombshell I had asked for a ceasefire and then suggested we make our way to the diner so I could clean up, yes, but mostly so it'd give me a chance to collect my thoughts. Which I'd almost managed to do by the time I sat down in the booth, but I still needed some fine-tuning. I knew I'd be better as soon I went back to the rooming house and slept for, oh, maybe three years or so but sleep would have to wait. There was still this teenage girl sitting across from me, drinking coffee and nibbling at a piece of cherry pie. She who I'd originally thought was a ghost. She who'd saved my bacon when it was roasting over the fire. She who, apparently, was the daughter of Adora Carmichael and Rolly Stevens.

"What?" she asked.

I'd been staring. "Sorry, shellshock."

"I still can't get over it. That guy was fixin' to rip out all your teeth."

"Before he called himself Quest, Janssen used to be a dentist, until he lost his license and went underground. Offered his services to the down-and-out under the guise of helping them but I think he got his jollies doin' it, the sick bastard. Probably liked the feeling of having them owe him, his army of society's rejects."

"That's bananas."

I had to agree with her, though I didn't even tell her about the really bananas part. How somewhere along the line, between my run in with Janssen and waking up half-buried in the sand at Kitsilano beach, I'd received a haircut. Close on the sides, a little bit off the top. I'd had to do a double take in the washroom mirror but it was true. My hair was definitely shorter than before and smelled faintly of pomade, underneath the overpowering ammonia of my new cologne, Eau de Seagull Shit. "Yeah, it's been one hell of a few days. I also have a metric ton of questions."

"Adora said that might happen. What you lack in looks and finesse you make up for in an admirable, if not dogged, curiosity. Like a basset hound."

I reached again into my inside jacket pocket. "Tell her I've got something in here for her as well."

Ellie grinned. "You betcha."

"But you don't call her 'mom'?"

"Not to her face, which really ticks her off. And that, Fitch, is what I call fun."

Fun, sure. Like mother like daughter.

"And she's okay with us discussing this?"

"I don't care if she is or not. My life."

"True. And I'm not above bribery, so tell you what? I get Glenda to make us a pot of coffee and leave it on the table and you tell me everything."

"No interruptions?"

"None."

"And I get to drink as much of the java as I want to?"

"Yup."

Ellie quickly drained what was left of her milky, sugary "coffee" and held out the empty mug for a refill. "Deal," she said.

12

DAYS PASSED. A new routine played over and over like the latest hit 45, in which the lyrics were simple and easily learnable and the melody was fairly annoying but also catchy, so that it looped in the head, lodging there like a tick burrowed into a dog. And the drums, the heartbeat, were steady and kept everything on track and on time. So that by the end of the song it was easier than not to lift the needle and place it back at the beginning. Familiarity. Comfort. Engaging with the "known" instead of the "unknown" being the best way not to leave any silence lying around. Because a silence bored is a silence asking questions, getting in your business, sticking its nose where it doesn't belong.

So, radio station DJ, play the song again. And again. On repeat. And the song was this:

1. Wake up in the middle of the night, covered in sweat
2. Check pulse—yes still alive
3. Vow to never fall asleep again because that way the nightmare about being eaten alive by people-goblins

can't come
4. Brew hotplate coffee, drink, repeat (helps with 3)
5. Sit in chair by window and wait for sunrise
6. Close eyes briefly only to be met with same nightmare
7. Revisit #3, realizing that the nightmare/flashback has followed you to the waking hours
8. Shiver
9. Sweat more
10. Shower
11. Brush teeth
12. Get dressed
13. Put one foot outside, say "Oh, hell no" and retreat back inside to the safety of your boarding house room
14. Wait for Ellie to come by with food from diner (which is always chicken noodle soup for some reason)
15. See #4
16. Sit in chair by window until sunset
17. Reaffirm #3
18. Fail at #3
19. Start back at #1

Sweating. The drug Janssen had slipped me while I was helpless in the dentist chair oozes out of my pores.

It oozes out neon green, purple.

Look down, no trace.

Crazy loses meaning in a world of crazy.

Sweating.

Fearing the memory flash of goblin maw, of green-yellow

mottled skin, a catalyst that would transport me beyond the void, to the other side, possibly never to return.

• • •

One afternoon—maybe a Tuesday, maybe a Friday (who could say, really, days of the week were such an arbitrary description of time anymore)—my landlady, good ol' Ms. Crawley, stopped by to say hello and spread her particular brand of cheer. She lived next door so it wasn't a long trip. Still, somehow, she was breathing a little heavy and slightly out of breath. Rather disconcerting.

"It stinks in there," she said, as I opened the door. Not sure if she noticed but I kept the chain on. Though not particularly worried my landlady was a goblin with a human skin disguise waiting to crack my bones open and suck the marrow, I was also willing to err on the side of caution. "You need to open a window now-and-then, Fitch."

"I'm trying to see who'll break first, me or the roaches."

She moved forward, closer to the gap in the door. Her breath was a bouquet of cheap sherry and nicotine. "Testy testy."

"Was there something else you needed…?"

"You've been on the hallway phone a lot lately, haven't you?"

"Guilty as charged," I said. Acting on a few suspicions and digging for the associated dirt helped pass the hours between night sweats and day sweats and those pesky in-between sweats. Like about Janssen and his history. Something about the way he'd said, "We don't like that" when I called him crazy got me wondering. Janssen was a slimy operator with a scaly exterior and the gift of the gab, not unlike a chatty lizard, so it was difficult to tell when strikes got through.

But I'd hit a sore spot, no doubt. I remembered how some of the Ontario fellas around the hobo camp where I first met Janssen used to call him the "Kingston Kook" when Janssen wasn't around. I'd always assumed it was because he'd spent some time in Kingston and was nuttier than a bowl of cashews but now I thought there might be a little more to it. "But with Mrs. Henry in the hospital for her bum ticker, I thought it best to maintain the status quo."

Winking, she said, "Well, you may be dialing out a lot, but what I don't hear is that phone ring much anymore. You know the call I mean. The one late at night. Your lady with the fancy dress and car. I mean, it's no wonder, Fitch. She's way outta your league. You look like a pile of moose dung these days."

"And your visits are like a ray of sunshine, I ever tell you that?"

Ms. Crawley lit a cigarette, took a puff and tilted her head up and to the side to exhale. I think it was supposed to be sexy. Uh oh. I sensed danger ahead. "I was pouring myself an afternoon libation and thought maybe you could use some company. Cooped up here in all day…"

Oh my. Rock say hello to Bottom. All I could stammer out was an eloquent, "Um…oh…uh…"

"Never really looked at you twice, truth be told, you were too young to know how to satisfy a real woman. But I've always been a sucker for a man gone to seed. I like 'em a little broken and scarred."

For once, I actually had no words. Not one.

— Good afternoon.
— Yes, hi, is this the Kingston Psychiatric Hospital?
— Yes.

— Fantastic. I'm calling about a possible former patient of yours. A "Copernicus Janssen" who may have been there a few years ago.
— May?
— Yes.
— I can't comment on any patients' status.
— But he was a patient there?
— That's not what I said.
— Oh.
— I can neither confirm nor deny any patient status over the phone. Are you a medical professional?
— Not in the classic sense, but I did get a paper cut the other day and miraculously survive.
— I'm sure your mother is very proud. Goodbye, sir.

— Hello?
— This Fitch?
— Yeah, that's me.
— It's Ronnie, from the Point Grey health club. You left a message for me saying you needed information and would make it worth my while.
— I did, yeah. You worked on September 10th last year, morning shift?
— You betcha. 5 a.m. to 1 p.m.
— Beautiful. That's the day a member, Rolly Stevens, slipped in the shower and ended up in the hospital.
— Oh yeah, I remember.
— Anything you can tell me about that day?
— What's in it for me?
— Do you like chocolate bars, Ronnie?
— You're kiddin', right?

— It depends.
— I like 'em, sure. But not as much as I like dough.
— Ah, a cookie man.
— So, you're a comedian, eh?
— I try.
— Try harder.
— A ten-spot.
— Make it a 20 and we're golden.
— You're killin' me, Ronnie.
— We're all dyin', Fitch, some us just get our questions answered while we do so.
— That's deep. Okay, sure, 20. I'll mail it.
— Your jokes are gettin' worse, Fitch.
— You don't trust me?
— Not one bit. Grace my palm with the dough and I'll call you back and spill the skinny. Until then, chow.

— Mr. Fitch?
— Yes.
— Thanks for waiting.
— Thanks for taking the time to look into this for me.
— My pleasure. Slow news day here today in Kingston. So tell me about this book you're writing.
— Book?
— The receptionist who transferred your call said you were working on a book.
— Oh, right. "My" book.
— About rogue dentists?
— Yeah, that's right. Big problem out west. Hordes of them roam the streets fillin' cavities and handing out lollipops to little kids.

— Really? Well, we did publish a story about a dentist offering some illegal services a few years ago. I pulled the edition from the archives.
— Let me guess: Copernicus Janssen.
— That's right. He was caught operating without a license and was known to pull teeth that didn't need to be pulled, particularly from the mouths of vagrants and alcoholics, to whom he offered his services for free. He ended up under psychiatric care.
— No surprise there.
— Can you imagine? The fear sittin' in that guy's dentist chair?
— Yeah, imagine that.

— Fitch, it's Ronnie.
— You got it?
— I did. You always get teenage girls to do your payoffs?
— Only when the eight-year-olds are in school.
— Yeah, a comedian.
— Okay, spill it.
— What do you want to know?
— Anything special about that day? Anything suspicious?
— Suspicious?
— Yeah. My theory is Rolly Stevens didn't slip and bash himself into a coma. He had a little help.
— That's not what the cop said.
— I'm an independent thinker, what can I say?
— Nothing I can remember, though I did check the register for ya. There was a square here that morning on a guest pass and he's never been back, not that I can

find.
— Oh yeah?
— Yeah. Signed in as Robert Smith.
— Million of those.
— True. But I remember this guy. He may have a common name but he was anything but common.
— How so?
— He was built like a concrete mixer, all neck.
— You don't say.
— Yeah, it started at his ears and went out from there.
— Interesting. One more thing.
— Better make it a two-dollar question, bud. The taximeter's at 18 bucks and I ain't in a generous mood.
— You said the cop didn't think there was any foul play.
— That's right.
— You recall the cop's name?
— Hard case. Worked more with his fists than brains. Mon-something.
— Montrose? Butch Montrose?
— Yeah, I think so. He looked like a bulldog.

Another afternoon—Tuesday, Sunday?—Ellie eyed the hot-plate java I was pouring for her and said, "And here I thought you looked bad before. Boy, was I wrong."

I stopped pouring and pointed. "There's the door, thanks for stopping by."

"Okay, okay, jeez."

I finished the pour and slid the cup over. "You're the second person to tell me that lately."

Ellie gave a knowing smirk. "Where there's smoke…"

"There's an ornery ostrich with his head in the sand wishing everyone would mind their own damn business?"

Ellie ignored me, cracked open the small carton of milk I'd put on the table, scooped up a few spoons of sugar from the bowl beside the milk and took a sip. "Anyway, I know you're bluffin'. I'm about the only friend you have right now."

Damn, just like her mom, a bullseye artist, a crack shot.

Ellie sat down and sniffed. "But at least you aired the place out. Smells better in here."

"I had a change of heart. The Ghost of Fitch's Future paid me a visit and I saw what awaited me if I didn't change my ways. And it was truly terrifying."

Standing there, at the door, being hit on by Ms. Crawley, I'd realized I'd hit a low point. The social misfit, loner, and woman whose apartment reeked of, whose very essence was that of cooked cabbage, called me out on my strange behaviour and thought I'd finally become attractive. After I'd escaped the hungry loop of her flirt rope by shutting the door in her face without another word, I knew it was time to shape up.

Now, watching Ellie, I sipped my coffee. Nothing like Glenda's heavenly brew but it was a temporary solution, a plan B. Something to tide me over until I was fit to be out in the world again. Ellie stirred more sugar in. She fidgeted. She said that next week was March break so she had some time to kill if I needed her to snoop around. I thought about it and decided no, bad idea. Then I thought about it some more and gave her a rundown, a few bills of folding money and said to take a cab. And don't get seen and don't take any risks.

Not the most responsible thing I'd ever done, asking a 14-year-old girl to be my eyes and ears on the outside. No, not even close. But less-than-comfortable times called for less-than-comfortable measures.

13

A WEEK, MAYBE TWO, after my involuntary dentist appointment, the hallway phone rang at 2 a.m. The ring sliced through the eerie quiet like a hot knife through butter. I sat up. I sighed. I got ready. Though I set the scene differently this time than ever before. I turned on all the lights. There wasn't an unlit bulb in the place. I got a pot of coffee going on the hotplate. Twenty minutes later, Adora opened the door. Her eyes glimmered: scotch and secrets, no doubt.

"Oh," said Adora, seeing me sitting in my chair, lit up like a deer in the headlights. "You're usually giving me the bedroom eyes when I walk in."

"We need to talk."

"This is new."

"Wouldn't you know but there's actually blood in my brain tonight."

She eyed me south of the equator then slipped off her heels near the door and tippy-toed over. She knelt and cupped me to check. "Hmm. True. I was kind of counting on your one-track mind tonight. Baby's got an itch."

I lifted her hand away. Adora was dainty but it took effort. My resolve to talk instead of rolling in the hay, once a concrete fortress, was now a small castle of sand and crumbling fast. "And I'd usually be happy to scratch."

"But…?"

"But tonight I'm a man with a mission."

"Indeed. And with a beard. What's with the Grizzly Adams look?" Of course, if she'd been talking with Ellie at all then she knew I'd been less than friendly with the outside these days and neglecting certain grooming habits. "Though it's a bit patchy here. And here. And over here." I brushed her hand away. She stood and pointed to the string of blinking red, yellow and green bulbs across the headboard. "Nice touch. But, Fitch, honey, Christmas ain't for months."

"What can I say, I'm in a festive mood."

Adora stood and sat on the edge of the bed, looking me straight in the eye, dead serious. "Or is it that you turned on every light you own because you think I'm dark as the night?"

That remark, plus the gaze with which she delivered it chilled me to the bone. She was right: I'd once believed her to be the bad apple that fell close to the criminal tree her father, Roosevelt, planted and leader to a gang of criminal clowns whose list of misdeeds could fill a novel. What I never really understood was if she was rotten to the core. Now it was time to find out for sure. I said, "I had a little chat with Ellie. She told me an interesting story."

Adora played it cool as ice. She opened her cigarette case and lit a stick like she was on stage, performing for an audience. Controlled, with purpose. "She didn't mention it."

"I got the Coles' Notes version. Boy meets Girl. Girl gets pregnant. Girl leaves days-old daughter with Boy's family because Girl didn't want the responsibility."

"Every story has its angles. Left out of Ellie's version is 'girl menaced in the hospital by a scary clown sent by her father with a clear message: return to the circus alone or else.'"

"You didn't tell her?"

"She won't believe me. Ellie's…stubborn."

"I said it before, I'll say it again: like mother like daughter."

Adora's perfect smoke rings were puffed out with enough patient, executioner-like expertise I feared they'd encircle my throat and tighten like the four floating nooses they were but instead they dissipated into the air. "You play poker, Fitch?"

"I've played. Most times it plays me."

"Well, you don't show all your cards until the end, right?"

"So this. Us. It's a game?"

"Isn't all of it?" she said, to which I shrugged, unwilling to commit. Damned if you do, damned if you don't. Adora cocked her head to the side inquisitively, another move I'd seen Ellie making. "So you tell me everything?"

She had me there.

"Okay," I said, "but wasn't that important scoop, you know, that her father, your ex, was Rolly Stevens, who I may or may not have indirectly accused you of murdering."

"Oh, you definitely did. And I definitely indirectly said I didn't."

"You said 'maybe,' as I recall."

"There were a lot of maybes being tossed around in that hospital room, including if you were going to lose that kidney."

"Because one of your clowns repeatedly punched the bejeesus out of it."

"Not mine. Daddy's."

"You say potato, I say…"

Another fury of smoke rings into the air. "Okay, then, so let's call the whole thing off."

I swiped an imaginary point in the air. "Okay, you know your Cole Porter, congratulations. But yes or no, the clowns did work for you after took over the family, uh, business?"

"Yes, true. And then I had to let them, uh, go."

"Oh, I remember. I still have those nightmares to contend with as well." And it was true. She may have saved the day, but Adora riding in on a stampeding elephant had nearly turned me into human paste. "It was definitely a terminal decision, you know, from a human resources standpoint."

She did a good Cheshire cat grin. "Maybe it was."

"Right, Adora Carmichael, my 'Maybe Baby.'"

"It seemed easier to work in misdirection. Plus, your mind was made up. You had your theories and it didn't matter what I said. I saw that."

"But you killed some clowns."

"The cops couldn't prove it. And if I did it was to help you. And me. They were vicious fiends and sizing my ship up for a mutiny. Slit my throat ear-to-ear in the process."

"And Moyer?"

"He decided to relocate after Ichabod and I had a serious chat with him about taking things that don't belong to him."

Ichabod was an old "friend," he of the small head and the pointy teeth, a former Dead Clown who survived Adora's culling by stampeding elephant because he was loyal to the boss not his fellow clowns. Now he was her occasional driver/bodyguard. And management at the supper club, way I heard. The kind of management that might prefer to use violence and intimidation as a motivational technique.

And Cleveland Moyer was the building manager that found the bag of money that Jim, the janitor, aka Buckles, the Dead Clown, had shot Adora's father for once upon a time. Last year, after the dust the stampeding elephant kicked up had settled, I'd found his Cadillac, bought with the stolen money, left in his driveway with the door open and a trail of blood leading to the street, where it abruptly ended.

I looked her dead in the eyes. "For real?"

She looked right back. "For real. He may have vamoosed with a bloody nose and an arm that didn't hang right but vamoosed he did. My parting gift was a bus ticket out of town, with one condition: it had to be used then. Get outta Dodge quick before I change my mind. He decided to take me up on my offer."

"Smart guy."

Adora laughed. "First time anyone called Cleveland Moyer smart, I bet. Cunning, maybe. But I'm smart."

"Oh yeah?"

"Yeah. And what I know, Fitch, is that you're rotting in this room like a piece of fruit that looks fine until you pick it up and see the mushy part where it touched the bowl."

I poked my side. "I'm mushy?"

She pointed to her head. "No, in here."

"Thanks."

"You're welcome. So let's do something about it. I know a place we can go and relax a little bit. Take the edge off."

"What, you're gonna whisk me away to a secret destination and ply me with booze?"

"Maybe. That a problem?"

I thought about it. "Nah, was only makin' sure."

• • •

So, like an egg cracked into a mixing bowl, not knowing if it'd end up scrambled or baked in a cake, I let myself be whisked. First, into the bathroom down the hall for a shower and a shave. Second, into a suit. Third, into the back of Adora's limo, with its tinted windows and seats that, if they could talk, would probably spin one hell of a yarn.

Ichabod, of course, was at the wheel. He nodded to me in the rearview and then raised the divider splitting the limo into two different worlds. The limo headed out of Gastown on Hastings Street, turned left on Cambie and made a right on Georgia. Destination: uptown.

As we went, my mind raced with theories and schemes. Last year several prominent businessmen with criminal ties to the Vancouver underworld had met with some outrageous bad luck. The get-dead-quick-and-in-the-shadows kind of bad luck. First, Rolly Stevens, then Salvatore Puccio, nightclub owner with a side business in sin, got hit by a laundry truck on Granville Street while out walking his beloved standard poodle in the early A.M. hours. Again, no witnesses except a stunned driver who said, according to newspaper reports, "I tell ya, that guy, he came out of nowhere." Back then I was in Private Eye mode and apt to tie everything up in a pretty bow, claiming it as Adora's ruthless power grab, a hostile takeover by her and the Dead Clowns, moving in on the local criminal brands to establish her own. Now I was beginning to wonder whose move it may have been, or if it was a move at all. Accidents did happen. Though I sensed a new player in the game and it wasn't Adora. It was my old "friend," Copernicus Janssen.

Ichabod turned the limo right off Georgia, onto Howe Street, then made a quick left into the alley behind the Georgia Hotel, steering us into a loading dock parking spot.

"We're here," said Adora, opening the door.

"Of course we are," I said. "You don't like front doors much, do you?"

Adora only smiled and made a motion like "you coming or what?" and then led us to a set of wide loading doors that were immediately opened by a large man in a tux who more resembled a concrete slab with arms and legs.

"Mrs. Carmichael," he said, nodding.

"Good evening, Charlie."

Unescorted, I followed Adora down a hallway to the service elevator, which we took to the top floor. The elevator opened into another hallway and after a series of rights and lefts, we were greeted by yet another concrete slab in fancy dress standing guard in front of yet another door, one with the muffled din of a bar in full swing behind it. I was near lost from all the twists and turns and half wished I'd put down some breadcrumbs in case I needed to find my way out.

"Your table awaits, Mrs. Carmichael."

"Excellent. Thank you, Anthony."

Anthony opened the door. I was right: the bar was hoppin', packed with cool cats and dashing dames. As soon as we stepped into the bar, a host spotted us and led us to a cozy little nook in the corner.

"Thank you, Pierre," said Adora.

"Of course, Mrs. Carmichael. The usual?"

"Make it two this time." Adora nodded to me. "And okay, one for him, too."

Pierre nodded and walked away.

"Charlie, Anthony, Pierre?"

"I might be a bit of regular here."

"You don't say."

"You'll see why in a minute."

I spent my minute watching the band working their way through a nifty rendition of recent radio hit, "Tequila," by The Champs. They knew their stuff and kept the dance floor sweaty and happy. As they segued into "Get a Job" by The Silhouettes, Pierre returned with two cocktails. But these were unlike any cocktail I'd ever had. Each glass looked like it contained a cloud floating in a hazy sky.

"Try it," said Adora.

The "cloud" tickled my nose but the booze went down smooth. "Yowza."

"It's the hotel's own concoction. They're cagey about the ingredients but I'm pretty sure it's gin and the 'cloud' is egg white sprinkled with grated nutmeg."

"Who knew I'd ever like an overcast day in a glass so much?" I took another sip and sat back, taking in the scene from our corner perch. The joint was alive, for sure. So was I, slowly returning to form. The music, the buzz of conversation, the booze, all playing a role in righting my ship, the one that'd listed to the side over the last days.

I thought about my calculations. Strange math but it added up. Hugo's father dies in a "fall," and Hugo becomes a shut-in still signing cheques but it's Janssen wielding the chequebook and being chauffeured around in the Brasher family automobile. Rolly gets the hard push from Janssen to sell the business, later "slips" in the health club shower and the tow truck company is then bought by a mysterious third party. And the way that tow truck driver tipped his hat to Janssen outside the warehouse…like a nod to the Boss, a King. Deference.

"By the way," I said, leaning over the table slightly and talking low, "I found out that a man that fits the description of Janssen's henchman, Reynold, was at the Point Grey health club that morning. And Butch Montrose, now head of Janssen's security, was the cop that investigated. I bet he smelled something fishy and sat on it, prepping an angle to hit Janssen from. Then, when Mrs. Brasher fell in his lap, he had everything he needed to shake the tree and see if some money fell out. It'd be quid pro quo. Butch eats what he knows, Janssen promises to feed him well in the future."

"Sounds like quite the conspiracy," said Adora, nodding

the kind of slow, deliberate nod that says, *Cough cough nudge nudge*. I'd been slow to the party but now that I'd arrived it made sense.

"You didn't kill Rolly, did you." I realized after I'd said it that it was a statement, not a question.

"Easy on the 'k' word, okay? Ears everywhere."

"Right, sorry. You didn't, uh, 'take him to dinner'?"

Adora shook her head. "I loved Rolly. But we were kids and it wasn't the right time. Probably never would've been."

"Some people shouldn't be together."

She looked me up and down. "I guess I don't learn, huh?"

"What, me?"

"You think we're a match made in heaven or hell?"

"Oh," I said, as surprised as a pig gettin' truffles when it thought all that was in the bucket was slop. "We're a match?"

"Enough to keep me lighting the fire when I don't know yet if one of us is gasoline. This last year, I've dated bankers and lawyers, gangsters and politicians and…"

"And…?"

"And I keep showing up to that fleabag room in that fleabag building in that fleabag neighbourhood."

"No doubt the stimulating conversation."

She laughed and "harrumphed" at the same time. Made for an interesting sound. Adora took a big sip from her cocktail. "I couldn't be a mother back then. I can barely handle it now."

"Ask for help."

"I am. But not for what you think. Because what I can handle even less than being a mother is that monster walking around. If you're thinking what I'm thinking then you're right. The dentist may not have done it with his own hands, but he's equally as guilty. He deserves to get taken out for 'dinner,' believe me. He did the same to Rolly, my daughter's father. And someone I used to love very much."

"So, what are you saying?"

"Get him. Janssen, Quest, whatever the hell his name is. Figure it out so I don't have to. I promised myself, for Ellie's sake. I'm worried that if I plan a meal on Rolly's behalf, it'll be a step too far. That I won't come back."

Knock me down with a feather, I was flabbergasted. I think it was the most honest thing Adora had ever said to me. Sap, tapped straight from the tree. The pure amber liquid clouded my judgment and made me feel noble. Truth was, I had to admit a little scheme had been brewing in the coffee machine of my mind over the last weeks and it was maybe, probably, ready for a pour. After all, I couldn't play the ostrich role forever. Had to get my head out of the sand and face this Janssen mess head on, or at least from an angle less likely to get me pulled through another window by Butch or my noggin twisted off by Reynold.

"Okay, fine," I said. "Let me give it a shot, my way. But it won't be dinner. More like a snack."

"As long as it's something."

"I'll need some things."

"Anything."

"For one, tomorrow's newspaper."

"That's it? You gonna roll it up and smack him over the head? I was hoping for something a little more, shall we say, painful."

"Don't, shall we say, worry."

"Okay. What else?"

"You know people, don't you?"

"I do, yes. Lots of them."

"Well, any of them happen to be pharmacists crooked like a nail been hammered in wrong?"

Adora looked at me funny.

"What?" I asked. "You know the type."

"Probably. I know another type, too."

"Yeah, that right? Devilishly handsome former unofficial private eye shut-ins with the wittiest of repartee and a hankering for another round of delicious cloud cocktails?"

"Yes, that kind."

"Sounds like a keeper to me, that kind of guy."

"We'll see."

Pierre walked by. I held up two fingers and winked. Adora grinned.

"Gettin' your mojo back?" she asked.

I returned a grin in reply and said, "Tell you what: whisk me back to my place after this and we'll find out."

14

THE NEXT MORNING, Adora was gone when I woke. No surprise, not for the reigning Queen of Stealthy Exits. In her place were two quarters on the pillow and a note that said, "Get your own damn newspaper, ya lazy sack of bones."

I set out to do just that. And this time, unlike the routine of the past several weeks, when my right foot hit the Gastown pavement I followed with the left. And I did that again and again until I was at the diner. Though I'd walked quick, head down, defenses up, in case of goblin attack. But all the humans seemed only human and going about their business and no one gave a rat's ass about me. Which was actually very comforting, to feel anonymous and unmarked. What I couldn't shake from the involuntary trip Janssen sent me on was that feeling of paranoia, of being watched, of every step being assessed for weakness, for when best to strike.

Inside the diner, it was mid-morning quiet, only a few souls nursing mugs of coffee, heads buried in their newspapers. The clock ticked. The grill hissed. Greek Benny stuck his head out the pass-thru window and dinged the bell for an order: two eggs over easy, hashbrowns and toast.

Glenda was happy to see me. She rushed over, gave me a big hug and sat me down at the counter like I was an invalid who recently returned from hospital. She took a seat beside me. "I'm so glad you're okay," she said.

"I'm hangin' in there."

"You had Benny worried. He asked after you every day."

"He did? Didn't know he cared."

"Well, the girl who picked up your soup said it was a real bad case of food poisoning, so he kept asking if you'd croaked yet and exactly how much of the cherry pie you'd eaten."

Ah, made sense. Greek Benny had a very active sense of self-preservation. As if on cue, he stuck his head out of the kitchen. I waved. He nodded once, a base acknowledgement, and grimaced.

"Look Benny," said Glenda, "Fitch's back."

"I can see that," said Benny.

"And he's fine."

"Hooray, it's a miracle. Shall I pop the Champagne?"

"No, just some more pie for me. Actually, I don't want to eat it now so if I could get it to go…"

"Go? Go where?"

"Out."

"Out?"

"Yeah."

"You wanna eat pie outside?" He narrowed his eyes at me. "You never get pie to go, why now?"

"And I have a special plastic container so if you could put it in there."

"Plastic container?"

"Yeah, I've told some other people about your delicious cherry pie and I want to get their professional, uh, I mean, 'expert' opinion."

"They really into pie, these friends of yours?"

"Not especially. They'll test, I mean, 'sample,' anything that could be contaminated. Contaminated with deliciousness, of course."

Benny finally got the joke, shook his head, called me an asshole, and ducked back in the kitchen. I fake wiped my eyes. "It's like old times. You guys are makin' me misty here. What'd I miss?"

"Well," said Glenda, "let's see. Lots of coffee and complaining, mostly. You know our clientele. But there was one good thing."

"Do tell."

"That guy that comes in here sometimes, what's his name? Barely a tooth in his mouth."

Sounded like a lot of the locals. I said, "You'll have to be more specific."

"Sips short dogs out of brown paper bags on the corner and has a cardboard belt."

Still, could've been a lot of guys but I nodded. I was pretty sure she meant Ricky Sims, aka No Teeth, who I'd last seen in line at the DSG warehouse. I went all goosebumpy. No ma'am, I didn't like the turn this conversation had taken. "Sure, I know who you mean. Seen him around."

"He came in for lunch the other day, all cleaned up and dressed half-respectful. Said he got himself a job washing windows and didn't order the usual soup paid for with a handful of pennies. This time it was a sandwich and he had folding money in his pocket. And a new set of fancy dentures to chew with. Real big and shiny white. Say, you okay, Fitch? You're shiverin' a little."

"Must be the air conditioning."

"It's not on."

"Oh, right."

40 NICKELS

"Cup of java to warm you up?"

I did the fist-guns-and-wink-yes bit, told her to please add two short stacks with extra syrup to that and it all felt enough like a normal life that I could almost forget my run in with the deranged dentist and his dandy psychedelics.

Almost.

Those goblins in the shadows, waiting for the night.

• • •

I had Adora's two quarters earmarked for the diner bill so the trick was waiting long enough on the right horse. And by horse I meant one of the two gents reading newspapers in the diner. I'd bet everything on the guy in the corner—sharp suit, salesman's briefcase, tapping his right foot—and eyed him on the sly like a bird keeps track of a worm. Sure enough, he packed up and rather than tucking the newspaper away, he left it on the tabletop. So nice of him. I quickly snatched the newspaper after the diner door chimed closed.

Get Janssen, she'd said. Whatever that meant to a woman like Adora, who may not have been the creature lurking under the bed I once thought but who knew her share of darkness and could bring it to your doorstep if you wronged her. Regardless, it was easier said than done. But I said I would give it a shot and named my requirements, after which she had a stipulation of her own.

"Promise me one thing," she said, as we drifted off to sleep.

"What's that?"

"I know you've had Ellie running some errands for you and that's fine. Hell, I forced her into your life and it's been good for her to get her mind off Rolly. But don't use Ellie for this, please. She doesn't need to know anymore about him and what he did. She loved her daddy very much and still believes it was an accident."

That said, and satisfied with my response, Adora closed her eyes.

As now, the diner door opened.

And in walked Ellie.

I'd nodded okay to Adora but had my fingers crossed.

• • •

We got down to business. Ellie ate pancakes. I skimmed the obits. I needed to figure out where Janssen would be at a given time, which was where the newspaper came in.

"So, this is about getting back at that dentist scummo that drugged you?" asked Ellie, chewing.

"Exactly," I said.

"Jeez, finally. I was beginning to worry I'd show up one day at your place and find that chair permanently fused to your ass. But why the doom and gloom section?"

"You mean the celebrations of life?"

"Sure, that."

I explained how I'd remembered seeing a newspaper open to the obituary section on Hugo's desk when I was "invited" in the house by Janssen and his goons. And that I'd noticed a red circle around several entries. Ellie nodded an "I see," and took a giant swig of coffee to wash down the last of her short stack.

"Easy on the bean juice there, eh?"

She fake shook her hand as she put the mug down. Coffee sloshed over the sides. "What, you think I might be over-doin' it a little?"

"Funny."

"Why's this guy so interested in funerals?"

"My guess is it's the rich widow angle, in particular. Easy prey. And he's a predator, no doubt. Smile that smile, spread that charm on real thick, then pass the donation plate and get more coin for the DSG coffer."

"Eww, lovely. But anything you saw circled would've taken place weeks ago."

"True," I said. Ellie was a sharp kid. I smoothed out the newspaper halved at the horizontal fold and tucked the left half under the right to isolate a small section of funeral notices. "But if I think like him I can see where this week's red circles would be."

"Clever."

"I have my moments."

"True, every dog has its day."

I tore the paper end off the wrapper of a diner straw, flipped it around and blew the paper tube her way. Bullseye, forehead hit. Her jaw dropped. She gave me "I can't believe you just did that" leer then returned the favour. And her aim was true. The plastic missile hit me in the chin.

"Oh, this means war," I said.

Straw Battle was as vicious as it was short. Soon spent shells of paper tubes lay everywhere, the straw jar sitting empty. No more ammunition. What we had plenty of were the curious glances, whispers, finger points and Greek Benny's furrowed brows as he glared at us over a plate piled with Salisbury steak, mashed potatoes and green beans.

Glenda wandered over. "You two about through?"

"Truce?" I put out my hand. Ellie shook it.

"Truce."

"Good. 'Cause we don't get another shipment of straws until next week. We get a run on milkshakes, you'll be hearing from me. And him." She hoisted a thumb at Greek Benny who was still glaring, but now there was a pastrami on rye with a side of fries added to the mix.

Tails between our legs, the hot course of combat adrenaline through our veins cooling, we scooped up all the paper tubes into a pile. It was a big pile.

"You were saying about the red circles," said Ellie.

"Yeah, you told me Janssen was holed up in the mansion, except for a few times when he left with his whole crew. Well, I think he was headed out to go fishing."

"Fishing?"

"Of sorts. At the funeral homes. Put out some widow bait on a hook and see if it gets a bite. It'd go something like how he knew the husband in business circles and it's such a loss, a shame, etc. and in times of sorrow nothing helps like a bit of the ol' TV medicine. And did they know they could help others see the light with only a small donation? I'm pretty sure he funded a large part of his whole 'religion' with widows' cash. And in Brasher's case, surviving heir cash."

"Crafty son-of-bitch."

"You allowed to curse?"

"You allowed to be so square?"

I mock tipped my hat to her. Touché. "You think your mom had us meet because she thought you needed a father figure or I needed some responsibility?"

"Definitely your problem. You're a mess, Fitch."

I shook my head, ouch, direct hit, and reached for new ammunition in what would undoubtedly be a hard fought Sugar Packet War, but Glenda interrupted, saying she'd meant to tell me that the Widow Brasher had been in the diner while I was home with food poisoning. "She was looking for you, Fitch. Last time a few days ago."

Guilt popped me a quick right hook. Snapped my head back. I tried to walk it off, no luck. Had to take a knee. I'd completely disappeared, hadn't I? Never even crossed my mind to follow up, to let her know I'd seen Hugo. He was not well and something hinky was going down for sure, but he was alive.

Ellie piped in. "Mrs. Brasher, that old lady with the chauffeur you told me about?"

"Yeah."

"I was going to tell you: I'm pretty sure I saw her car drive through the gates of that big house last night."

"You didn't take the tow truck, did you?"

"You think I'm an amateur? No, a cab, like you told me to."

"She come out?"

"Beats me. I had to make like a tree and leave so I could get back home before mommy dearest got there. She's got me on a tight leash these days."

"Honey," said Glenda, "you okay? Isn't that too late to be staying up before school?"

"Oh, I don't go to school anymore. Fitch said it was a waste of time, that I'd learn a lot more working for him."

"Fitch!" Glenda hit me on the arm with a menu.

"What?" I said. "I never."

Ellie winked, full of mischief. "I'm busting your balls. No school this week so I've been helping out ol' Fitchy here."

Glenda hit Ellie on the arm with a menu, twice.

Ellie shot Glenda a wounded look. "What'd I do, lady?"

15

— Taffy, good buddy.
— Hey, Fitch.
— Long time no talk.
— I guess. Listen, I—
— What gives? You don't sound your usual jovial self. Bad time for a chat?
— Yeah, I'm a little stressed. Vacation starts today. Bahamas.
— By yourself?
— Nah, with the wife.
— Oh. Still should be fun.
— Yeah, if we can get to the airport.
— What do you mean?
— Ah, my no-good cousin just called to say he can't give us a ride to the airport no more. His appendix or something. Being rushed to the hospital yadda yadda. I swear that thing's ruptured a few times already.
— Can't you take a cab?
— Nah, the wife hates to fly and thinks if a stranger

drops us off we're more likely to snuff it in a crash. I can't figure it, but it's always got to be someone we know.
— Taffy. Buddy.
— Yeah?
— Come on.
— What, you?
— Yeah, of course. Anything for an old friend.
— You serious?
— Absolutely. Except I only got the tow rig, so I'll have to use your car.
— Fitch, you're a lifesaver. Three o'clock, okay?
— I'll be there.

The drive to the airport was uneventful, as far as traffic went. As far as the mood in the car, it was a battlefield and I had to keep my head low so as not to get hit by a stray bullet. Taffy and his wife were the kind of career soldiers that wore camouflage and hid in bunkers and sniped at each other over familiar territory that made precious little sense to anybody else.

"You said you packed it."
"You didn't pack it?"
"You said you would."
"I never."
"You did."
"You didn't even use it last time."
"Well, what if I want to this time?"
"Then why didn't you pack it?"
"I asked you to."
"No, you didn't."
Their war was truly hell, endless and circular in nature. I

probably didn't help matters much when, in the few silences there were, I shared lurid details from an article about plane crashes I'd read a few months back. Taffy kept shooting me stern glances from the front passenger seat. "Shut up, Fitch," he'd say, low, under his breath and then scramble to interrupt with a random observation, anything to steer the conversation in a different direction, far away from his wife's flying phobia.

"Well, will you look at that coat she's got on…"

"On vacation for ten minutes and he's already lookin' at other women. Wait until we get to the beach."

"I'm not lookin' at her I'm only sayin' it's a nice coat."

"So you don't like any of my coats?"

"Of course, but you don't have one like that."

"And why's that?"

"Let me guess: because I don't buy you one."

"No, because I'm not a whore."

It was good times.

So good that when I pulled Taffy's car up to the departure's drop-off he looked like he already needed a vacation from the vacation. I was pretty satisfied with my efforts on that front. Taffy took all the bags out of the trunk, then leaned in the window and handed me a two-dollar bill.

"Be a pal and top it up, okay? That way when we get back it's a full tank."

"Pook," I said. "You can count on me."

"Thanks, Fitch. And be care—"

I didn't hear the rest. I was too busy popping the clutch and speeding away with a screech of tires and a plume of exhaust. Frankly, I'd been surprised Taffy let me use his car again, what with our history. But I'd been lucky and caught him at an opportune moment when his need was big and his options were few.

40 NICKELS

So, yes, Taffy, you can count on me…to do the opposite.

I drove the car for another two hours, revving the engine, peeling the tires, having a blast, until the engine sputtered to a stop on Royal Avenue in The Royal City, New Westminster. I parked it best I could, got out, walked three blocks to the nearest payphone, flipped through the yellow pages hanging there and dialed the number for A-One Towing, Rolly's old company. A few minutes later and the dispatcher said she'd send someone right out. I walked back to Taffy's car, enjoying the cool evening air and the feel of pavement under my feet. My recent stint indoors hadn't been good for my constitution or my waistline and the ol' 1-2-right-left felt good, redeeming.

As I reached the car, I checked the scene. Sure, I could work with it. I ruffled my hair, undid a few buttons on my shirt and loosened my tie. I took the money, including Taffy's two-dollar bill, out of my wallet and tucked the bills into my sock. I reached in the window and flicked on the headlights and sat on the curb, at the edge of the light, knowing it would make me look even more pathetic and desperate. I put on my best forlorn face and waited.

Five minutes later, the tow truck pulled over in front of Taffy's car and the driver stepped out. He was a little shorter than me, wearing overalls shiny and stiff with grease and oil and had a peaked cap perched on his head. Said his name was Tucker and asked if I was okay. I muttered a quiet "Depends who you ask" and played the part. I had my head in my hands. I was losing. Life was winning. He seemed to buy what I was selling and hooked up the car with practiced efficiency.

"If you just sign here," he said, approaching with a clipboard.

"About that."

"Buddy, come on. Dispatcher said you'd be paying cash."

I turned out empty pockets, an empty wallet. "I got nothin', pal. I'm tapped. Ran out of gas and can't afford to get home."

"You know I gotta take this to the yard now, right?"

"I know."

"You can get your sled out when you got the dough. The bill's gonna be steep though."

"Sure, I love running uphill. Fall down, you get to the bottom real quick."

"Sorry, pal."

"Not your fault I'm a loser on a losin' streak."

"The least I can do is get you home."

"How about my Gastown local? I got a tab I can pile another whisky onto before it topples like a house of cards."

He thought about it. I kept my head down while he did so. "Into Vancouver? Sure, why not? I could use a drive. And if you want to try and drown your sorrows with booze it's no skin off my nose. I ain't your mother. Hop in."

I got in the front seat and shut the door. He got in and started driving, turning right on 8th Street and heading us back towards Vancouver.

"That Rolly was quite a character," I said. "May he rest in peace."

"That he was," said Tucker. "You knew him?"

"Nah. Only by reputation. Who bought him out?"

"Some outfit out of Manitoba. Fell Brothers, Inc." He gave me a side glance then looked back at the road. "You a reporter or somethin'? Awful curious."

"Sorry, pal, didn't mean to bend your ear so it hurt. Only makin' conversation. Along with no gas money, no more real friends anymore either." I stared out the window. I played the sad sack. I let him bring it up like I suspected he would.

40 NICKELS

"Havin' a rough go of it, eh?"

"Buddy, you ain't kiddin'. There is not a defeat I can't snatch from the jaws of victory these days." I listed my recent accomplishments: broke, no job, no prospects, ditched by fiancé for a rich lawyer-type.

We drove in silence for a few minutes. Then he reached over, cracked open the glovebox and handed me a pamphlet from a stack of pamphlets inside.

"Listen," he said, "I can't vouch for these people, but I hear good things. They might be able to help you."

I opened up the pamphlet. It was slick and glossy, professionally done.

Becoming a Disciple of the Sacred Glow means becoming part of our family.
A family that watches TV together, stays together.
Let the warmth of the glow soothe your troubled soul.

I wanted to shout, "Bingo!" but played it cucumber cool.

• • •

I had Tucker drop me off a block down from the Four Corners. Time to stretch my legs, my brain. I told him my local was around the corner and hopped out at a red light. He wished me good luck and drove away fast on the green, Taffy's car trailing behind, leaving me alone on the sidewalk. Tucker wasn't a bad guy. Only trying to do his job, make a buck or two while he did so and follow the new regime's orders. He told me there was a cash bonus for any recruit that came to a DSG meeting and said a certain driver referred them. Said it made him uncomfortable but who couldn't use some more cash, right, buddy? I couldn't disagree with him. Had it worked out another way, I would've called the number on the pamphlet and checked out a meeting. Let Tucker get his reward and see what Janssen was up to. But part of my "let's empty out Taffy's gas tank" adventure had been a quick drive past the Brasher warehouse and it was locked-up tight from the looks of it. I didn't dare get closer, not yet, but it seemed Janssen and his cronies had gone to ground.

I wondered if it was some other play? Did he sense me out there, looking for him? It was impossible to say. Certainly, I knew some things but not enough to hurt him. Not really. I had pieces of ragged supposition chipped from a square block of wild imagination. He had two brute henchmen and a network of tow truck drivers and former winos turned upstanding card-carrying members of the Disciples of the Sacred Glow. What I couldn't figure, other than the God complex he clearly possessed, was what purpose the whole racket served. Damn sure had to be easier ways to be admired and make a buck at the same time.

Instead of heading for home, I decided to slap some shoe leather against Gastown concrete, a tried-and-true tradition. My head was spinning like a top and a walk usually helped it slow to a stop so I didn't get too dizzy. And I was in no rush to get home. I had time. My main play on the Janssen front had a complete script but I needed the curtain to open and the spotlight to shine. Having identified three funerals in the obituaries I thought Janssen might be likely to show up at to perform his schtick, the next part was competing in the waiting game. I'd struck out so far and the last funeral of the three was tomorrow afternoon, so until then I had nowhere in particular to be.

My walk brought me to a slice of city where waves from the boats in the Burrard Inlet lapped up against concrete barrier wall and the blue-and-red flashing lights from the roof of the police cruiser cast an eerie spell. The crime scene was taped off and I stood as close as I could get, among a small group of night owl gossipy types. True to form, they were very informative. It seemed a body had just been pulled from the water after getting caught up in the net of a fishing trawler. Seemed it had probably been in the water for a couple of days.

"Homicide?" I asked the guy closest to me.

He nodded and said he overheard whispers that the corpse had been ventilated several times post-mortem with a blade so it wouldn't be a floater.

My mouth went dry. "Gruesome business."

"You said it, pal. And someone ripped out all his teeth, too. Way I heard it, he's got nothin' but gums and exposed nerves."

A plainclothes cop flashed a badge our way. "Hey, lookie loos, move on, why dontcha? Police business."

I moved on but only as far as the nearest alley mouth, where I lurked, seeing what I could see. It seemed while I was waiting for the right funeral, Janssen was making one of his own, one that served his ends, whatever those may be. I caught a glimpse of the ventilated corpse as they removed it from the water and it sure looked a lot like the guy I'd happened to sit next to at the warehouse when I first discovered the DSG and Janssen as Quincy Quest. The nervous guy. The one sitting right beside me, who definitely would've heard me call the man billing himself as Quest "Janssen" just like Mrs. Brasher said.

I wasn't a betting man, per se, but my money would be on him having been the old lady's "molar." Ironic, considering he had none anymore. I shuddered at what his last moments must've been like. Janssen was getting more vicious, more brazen. But was he spinning out of control or in a controlled turn, getting ever closer to his goal?

And then there was the fact that Mrs. Brasher had gone

into the mansion and not been heard from again, at least as far as I could find. I'd swung by the Sylvia Hotel on my way to New Westminster and they said she'd checked out several days ago. But according to the front desk the guy that checked her out must've been a new assistant of hers because it wasn't the chauffeur and he didn't seem to know much about Mrs. Brasher. Taffy's car idling outside to burn more gas, I'd quickly asked, "This new assistant wear a Fedora, look like a bulldog and have a limp?" and the desk clerk nodded.

Now, watching the cops zip the body bag closed, I gulped. Janssen was removing rotten teeth, both figuratively and literally. Was I next?

16

THE CABBIE GAVE ME A QUIZZICAL look through the rearview mirror when I told him Shaughnessy and to make it snappy. "Nice neighbourhood," he said, obviously not thinking I belonged south of Broadway.

"It's okay," I said, winking. "If you don't mind tiny houses."

"Oh yeah, you're Richie Rich, huh?"

"Can't you tell?"

He lifted his head to get a more comprehensive look in the rearview. "In them rags, no."

"How do you think I got so rich? By not spending dough on fancy clothes, that's how."

"You don't say."

"I do say. Everything's invested in the market. Bulls and bears, you bet."

The cabbie said something about me only lookin' like I had potatoes in a vegetable market but it was mostly under his breath so I didn't press him for clarification. He was not impressed by my financial jargon. Though what he lacked in imagination he made up for with an extremely heavy lead foot. Plus, he must've been colour blind because several of those lights were extremely yellow. But who was I to judge? We made it to Shaughnessy in record time.

I had him turn right off Granville Street on to 33rd Ave and told him here was good. I handed over the fare. He made a sour face.

"Now I know you're loaded," he said.

"Oh yeah, how's that," I asked, one foot out the back door.

"Because you must be savin' a lot of dough there, too. You tip for dog shit, Jack."

I stepped out. The cab sped off.

I walked the remaining blocks, approaching the Brasher mansion from the side, hidden from view by the giant hedge surrounding the property. I'd learned from my past indiscretion of parking a tow truck with my name on it down the street and hoped this venture would be more on the sly side. Though I was counting heavily on Janssen's continued belief in my stupidity and pigheadedness in order to pull this caper off.

Until earlier today, I'd been zero for two on funerals and hoping the third time was a charm. And it was. Twenty minutes ago, Ellie had called me to say, yes, Janssen and his doggies, Butch and Reynold, had shown up at the funeral home in Hugo's Lincoln Continental. Wouldn't sound like much to an outsider not in the know, but for me it was headline material and exactly the news I was waiting to hear.

"No one's sticking with the car? No driver?"

"Nah, the one with no neck drove and they all went inside a few minutes ago."

"Fat city. So you know what to do?"

"Have Ichabod tow the Lincoln." I'd asked Ellie if she knew anyone who could help and Ichabod was the first name off her lips.

"He know how to tow a car?" I asked.

"I'll run him through it," said Ellie. "Not to worry."

"Make sure and scoot down in the seat. No need for you to get mixed up in this."

"Get? Aren't I already? By the way, my mother kinda hates you right now."

"She found out?"

"Yeah. But she knew she'd never convince me not to go, so instead, once she found out Ichabod was going with me, she okayed it."

"Phew."

"So, don't get caught but do try and make enough of a scene that they see our rig, the one with your name on it?"

"Exactly."

"Do we need their car or is this to piss them off?"

"The latter, mostly. And what do you do when that happens?"

"We drive like hell and stash the car somewhere in the sticks."

"You're a star."

"Two weeks and this is what you came up with, huh? Plan A?"

"And B and C."

"And I'm fourteen years old, you know that, right?"

"But you've got the resourcefulness and the coffee habit of a 40-year-old."

Ellie grumbled a "Sure, whatever you say, daddio" and hung up the phone.

I hightailed it to a cab and now here I was, about to sneak in the Brasher mansion knowing the master and his hounds were away for at least an hour or so. Maybe more, considering they'd have no car to drive home.

I needed an entry point and figured the rear of the

property might be the best chance. I walked slowly along the sidewalk—whistling, nothing to see here, simply a guy with no money in clothes and all in the vegetable market going about his day—until I saw a small gap in the hedge. Not much of one, merely a glimpse of light on the other side. It would have to do. I knew success would hinge on a combination of will and velocity. I took a two-step windup and bolted for the gap, crashing past branches, leaves and several thick spider webs, only disturbing a scurrying animal or three on my way through.

I stumbled out the other side of the hedge at the end of a yard that could've been an orchard had it wanted to work a little harder. The nearest tree provided shelter while I waited for any sign that my presence had been noted. Nothing happened and a furtive glance at the mansion windows told me only that the inhabitants did not like light one bit. Everything was sealed shut. Perfection. Still, caution was warranted so I crept tree to tree until I was at the rear of the massive structure.

One locked door and three shut windows later, I was crawling through an open window in front of a very prickly rose bush and very gracefully knocking over a pile of tin cans with my feet as I dropped down from the window ledge.

Wait a second: tin cans?

My eyes slowly adjusted from bright sun to dim lighting. I looked down and, yes, a pile of cans, placed right under the windowsill of the room I'd entered the hard way. Upon closer inspection it was a laundry room and the cans were for corned beef, baked beans and peas.

Thud clink.

The sound was coming from down the hallway.

"Oh shit," I said, under my breath.

Thud clink.

The sound was getting closer. The steadiness of it chilled me to the bone.

Thud clink.

Very close now.

Thud clink.

Frozen, I watched as a knight filled the doorway, sheathed head-to-toe in shiny armour. Probably an expensive get up but what had all of my attention was the very large sword the knight raised and pointed in my direction.

"That looks sharp," I said.

The knight nodded, said nothing.

"And that suit must be heavy."

Again, nothing, just a *thud clink* as the knight stepped closer.

It was all too familiar. Last year, neck deep in dead janitors and Dead Clowns, I'd followed up a lead on an unrelated insurance fraud case. Bartell Rightly was under investigation but had disappeared, until I tracked him to a remote cabin deep in the woods of Surrey. Well, he did more of the tracking because as I watched the smoke curl out of the chimney, thinking my rabbit was inside, he was creeping up behind me. I didn't realize until he sneezed and I turned around to see him dressed up in his military best and pointing a large rifle at my face. I'd thought Bartell was going to punch my ticket with a few slugs to the cranium but he smacked me with the butt of the rifle instead. Gave me a one-way ticket straight to the city of Sore Jaw in the country of Knocked Out.

Now, though, I feared there was only one course of action the knight wanted to take and I liked my intestines where they were, inside, doing intestine things.

Thud clink.

"Hugo, you don't want to do this." Hearing his name

stopped him in his tracks. The sword stayed raised but he took one hand off the hilt and tipped up the face protector.

"They said I shouldn't talk to you. But that I should protect this house at all costs. They called you an infiltrator. They said you wanted to turn the TV off, kill the glow."

"They?"

"Mr. Quest, Mr. Montrose."

"And let me guess, Reynold was nothin' but grunts."

Hugo nodded. "They're my family now."

"What about your mother? She was here yesterday."

"Yes, she was. She wouldn't relent, she never does, so Mr. Quest thought it a wise choice to let her in, to see that I was fine. I tried to make her believe, but she wouldn't listen."

"Where did they take her, Hugo?"

He pointed. "Out the back door. To the garage."

"Can I see?"

"I'm not sure. I was told not to leave the house or to let you live if you came knocking."

"Tell ya what: let's go look at the garage, you can stab me later."

Hugo thought about it. I wasn't sure if the longer he considered the better for my guts remaining where they were or not. Eventually, satisfied, he muttered, "Okay, this way."

Inside the huge garage, there were two cars: a maroon Ford in decent condition and an impeccably shiny Rolls Royce the colour of expensive, very expensive.

"That's mother's car," said Hugo, pointing to the Rolls. "She never walks."

"So you mean it's a little odd it's here and she's not?"

Hugo didn't answer. He didn't have to.

I checked out the Ford first. The exterior may have been okay to look at but the interior was a disaster. Candy bar wrappers, cigarette packs, clothes strewn everywhere and what appeared to be small, jagged rips in the seats.

"That's Butch's car," said Hugo.

"Yeah? He own a tiger?"

"No, a house cat. It's inside now, hiding probably. That thing's scared of its own shadow."

I opened the passenger side door and rooted through the glovebox. Insurance papers listing the car under Butch's name, a few city maps, an empty Oh Henry! wrapper. The usual. I moved on to the Rolls. I suppose it was okay, if you liked driving around in a luxurious tank. I opened the door. Mrs. Brasher's lilac perfume hit me like a freight train. It was definitely her car. By the time I got to the rear, the trunk area, I could still smell the lilacs but there was also a bad smell underneath. The stink of rot.

"There a fight? When your mother was here?"

"No, not at all. My mother was displeased but she's usually that way. It was all quite cordial. Mr. Quest had me explain that everything was fine and that it was my choice not to leave the house and sign the warehouse over to the Disciples of the Sacred Glow. Mr. Montrose even offered to help my mother to her car."

"Oh, did he now?"

Thud clink thud clink.

Hugo stood beside me now, sword at his side. He stared down at the trunk. "No," he said.

"It might be, Hugo."

"No."

"Don't open that trunk, okay? Trust me."

"It can't be. Not her, too. Not…"

I looked at Hugo. He didn't look so good. Probably roasting alive in that armour, for one. Throw in whatever drug cocktail he was on and it was no shockeroo he was woozy and off balance. Sure enough, ten seconds later, he was wobbling back-and-forth, each wobble getting increasingly large, as his eyes rolled to the back of his head.

Thud clink.

The Knight of Shaughnessy fainted.

He went *crash*.

• • •

Not knowing how long I had until Hugo woke up, and whether or not he'd want to turn me into a human pincushion when he did, I decided it'd be best to stay on track and not treat the Brasher abode like a museum. Which would be very easy to do. The place was a showroom, an ode to wealth gone overboard. Paintings. Statues. Giant vases. Many precious objects behind glass and putting your nose up against it to take a look left a smudge where no smudge had gone before. But that was the old days, the days of butlers and maids. Now, the shine had worn off. A layer of dust coated everything and the inside of the house smelled like what I imagined a thousand burps blown into a glass jar and stored on a shelf for a decade would smell like.

Made sense, though, considering I knew Hugo had let the maid go and now had three new male houseguests who must've been feral chimpanzees by the looks and smell of the house. Dirty dishes piled in the kitchen like mountains in a range. Fingerprint-smudged highball glasses, beer bottles and cans of open food with spoons stuck in the jellied muck littered the living room. Dust bunnies nearly the size of actual bunnies observed from the corners and a layer of grime and stink coated everything.

I quickly made my way through the main floor of the house to the study. The room seemed exactly as it was the day Janssen had tried to bribe me into silence, if not a piece of the cult guru pie. But I wasn't interested so he'd tried the usual way: dentistry and drugs. I got lucky and escaped. Now I was back to take a little revenge and maybe right a wrong or two.

I sat down at the desk and opened the drawer. The way Janssen loved this room and had taken ownership of it suggested to me that if there were any damning documents to be found they would be here, not the warehouse. And I wasn't right but I wasn't wrong. No smoking gun or bloody knife but there was a sheet of paper in the drawer that listed Hugo Brasher and Copernicus Janssen as co-owners of Fell Brothers, Inc. According to Tucker, they'd been the outfit to buy A-One Towing after Rolly's incident. Two "falls": Peter Brasher and Rolly Stevens. Now, Fell Brothers, Inc. Janssen was having a great ol' time, wasn't he?

I put the sheet of paper back where I found it and rifled around some more. Most of the documents pre-dated Janssen's move-in and were old Brasher Industries forms and Brasher house receipts. Snore-fest. Plus, I had another mission and the clock ticked-tocked. Better hurry and get down to the most important task:

There, on the pedestal, where Janssen had left them after showing off, were the 40 nickels. I breathed deep. It was happening. I grabbed the roll of coins and gripped them in my palm. Finally, they were back in my possession.

A movement caught my eye, in the doorway. I turned. A cat was staring at me, a calico cat to be more exact. A calico cat I'd seen before.

"Nah, couldn't be," I said, slowly reaching for my wallet so as not to disturb my new buddy. But the cat didn't care at all about me and was seemingly undisturbed by anything as he methodically splayed his legs and groomed his crotch in a narrow ray of sunlight on the hardwood floor. I unfolded the sheet of paper crammed in my wallet. It was Billy's missing cat flyer. I compared the photo to the cat in front of me.

"Yeah, it is. Holy shit. Mr. Jangles?"

The cat meowed.

17

THEY BRACED ME AT DUSK in the alleyway behind my rooming house. Reynold and Butch stepped out to block the back door as I was about to enter. Janssen waltzed up behind me, emerging from the cover of a garbage bin. Fitting.

"If there's one thing you can count on in this life it's a filthy rat returning to its filthy nest," he said, very pleased with himself and wanting the world to know it. "You think I didn't plan for you trying to sneak in?"

No, Janssen, I thought to myself, I'd been counting on it. But no need to tip my hand so I played it up and said, "Golly gee willikers, guess I got out thunk."

"It seems so. Reynold, let's show Fitch how we feel about him having our car towed, shall we?"

Reynold walked forward. I kicked him square in the balls. A good strike, too. Somehow he took it and only grimaced slightly. Tough son-of-a-bitch. He held up one finger. He was giving me one more shot. So I did the ol' point-over-there-what's-that? bit with my left hand, wound up with the right hand, waited for him to turn his head back, and slugged him square in the jaw.

That didn't go so well either.

Several bones in my hand broke like glass, maybe all of them. My hand was a bowl of Rice Krispies: snap, crackle, pop. And what gives? A punch that should've swiveled Reynold's head around like a spun top, barely registered more than a little flick to the side. Like hitting a brick wall with a bowl of Jello. It was that damn neck.

Reynold grunted a "That all you got?"

"That would've been harder," I said, trying to shake out the agony, "but I had to spend a few of those nickels along the way." The half-depleted roll of coins rolled out of my injured hand onto the alley concrete.

Janssen recognized them. He gasped. Reynold bent down, picked up my nickels and handed them to Janssen. Then he enclosed my hand in his mitt and squeezed, real hard. Bones, already shattered, turned to dust.

I screamed.

Reynold grunted.

Butch laughed.

Janssen said, "Yes, that's for the car, now what to do about these precious nickels you stole from my office? Butch, you have a score to settle with Mr. Fitch for dislocating your kneecap. Maybe you have something in mind?"

Butch limped forward, still favouring the wheel I'd kicked out of place. The nasty look on his face said Janssen was right. Butch was full of bright ideas. The knife he removed from his boot top said he'd decided on one in particular.

"Okay," I said, "let's be civil about this."

Janssen shook his head with mock sincerity. "If only, my old friend. The train we're on passed civility many stops ago. Now, I'm afraid, there's only one stop left."

I put up my left hand to stop Butch. "Fine, the wrecked

wheel I can take my lumps for, but don't stick me over some lousy nickels. I didn't spend them, Janssen, how could I? They're sacred. And in my pocket, in an envelope. Look for yourself."

Janssen eyed me suspiciously then reached into my jacket pocket, removing a white envelope. He shook the envelope, listening for the sound. The nickels answered back. "Of course, how could you? These coins mean as much to me as they do to you, don't they?"

"Well, I did steal them in the first place."

"Reynold, help me, will you? Butch, you keep an eye on our friend. But don't take any drastic measures quite yet."

Butch seemed disappointed but nodded in agreement.

Janssen shook the loose nickels from the envelope out into his hands. He cupped them in his palm. He brought them to his nose. He sniffed. He gave a satisfied "Ummmm." He put on a show. Personally, I loved it. It was more than I could've ever hoped for. I was the happy fisherman with a good piece of bait in the water and about to reel in a catch, hook, line and sinker. I had to contain myself not to shout for glee when Janssen dropped the nickels in Reynold's cupped hands and the henchman held them while he carefully, one-by-one, placed them back in the roll with the other nickels. It's what I wanted to happen but I needed to slow down the proceedings, distract him a little bit.

"Nickel by nickel, eh, Janssen? Like scamming hobos for a percentage of their wages?"

Janssen stopped and turned to me. "You figured that out, did you? Well, what was I supposed to do? Beautiful new teeth like that don't come for free. Call it a lifelong re-payment plan."

"And they default on the loan and you take your teeth back."

"What good would my name be if a broken contract didn't come with a penalty?"

"Slick. From hobos to rich widows, there wasn't a pocket you weren't willing to dip your hand in was there?"

"As you said, Fitch, 'nickel by nickel.' It adds up. Only 40 nickels and you have two dollars." Janssen turned back to Reynold and got back to the task at hand.

I turned my attention to the bulldog giving me the eye daggers. "This is riveting stuff, ain't it, Butch? They do a Saturday matinee?"

"Shut yer mouth, Fitch."

"Oh, the doggie talks."

"Woof woof."

"You know who else talks? Hugo. Not to me, of course. No, he was too busy walking around the house talking to a Mr. Jangles."

That got Butch's attention. "Say that again."

"Yeah, he had a bunch of tuna cans open all over the house and was looking for Mr. Jangles. A cat, I assume?"

"Yeah, my cat."

"Ooh."

"What?"

"Nevermind. I'm sure he wouldn't…would he?"

"Do what?"

"Nah, he probably wouldn't. Be a stretch, even for him."

"Spit it out, Fitch, while you still have a tongue."

"Okay, I don't know for sure, so don't quote me on it, but I think he was looking for this cat because he wanted to eat it. I shit you not. Said he was tired of canned food and wanted some real meat for a change. Hugo flipped his lid, me thinks. Wasn't even going to cook the cat from the sounds of it."

Butch went green. "You hear that, sir? What've you got him on? He capable of that?"

40 NICKELS

Janssen dropped the last coin in the roll and folded the formed end of the coin wrapper over. The 40 nickels were back together once again. "Hmm, let's see. I have been experimenting with some different doses lately. Hugo's been showing an increasing tolerance to my custom drug cocktail and I need to keep him obedient and signing those cheques for the near future, in order for the next part of the plan to come to fruition. I suppose the occasional setback could be a possibility."

I decided not to mention that Hugo was currently in full knight get up and wielding a large sword. And maybe still unconscious. Let that all be a nice surprise.

Butch turned back to me. "When was this?"

"'Bout a half hour ago."

"There's still time. Sir?"

Janssen sighed. "Fine, Reynold can take over. You go back to the house and check on Hugo."

Butch handed the knife to Reynold and scampered off, favouring the knee I'd dislocated from its socket. A proud moment, one of my greatest accomplishments. I heard Butch reach Hastings and begin to shout for a taxi.

One scumbag down, two to go.

"Well, that settles it," I said. "Doggies do love cats."

Reynold began to giggle.

• • •

The dosed nickels had been the bait. Expensive bait. Cost Adora a loan repay plus the vig. I'd asked for a crooked pharmacist and got a pharmacy school dropout instead. He was the brother of her new head chef. Adora overheard some kitchen chatter one night as the head chef told the sous chef about his fuck up of a brother, Stanley. Smart as a whip, kid prodigy, but dumb in a way that boggled the mind. Got kicked out of pharmacy school for selling scrips. Reckless, too, and not especially known for his impulse control, not when he was on roll, when the dice were hot hot hot. Seems he'd had a wild night out at an underground gambling den in Chinatown and got into some scary Triad boys for 300 scoots he didn't have. The due date on the loan was fast approaching and they were making their presence known, showing up at the bookstore where he worked and leaning up against a lamppost across the street when he left his house in the morning.

So Adora intervened, paid off the Triad on his behalf and gave me the kid's name and number. Said he'd be very motivated to help. And he was. Stan shook my hand and invited me into his kitchen for a chat. He dug my plan right away. He was hip to the scene. He was drug savvy and a drug den dabbler. But he didn't think western pharmaceuticals were the way to go. No, he spent six months last year deep in the Northwest Amazon stripped to the skivvies, living in a hut, licking hallucinogenic frogs, sipping root teas that'd make you see God and being ritually scarred in front of by the village elders.

I said, "Cool, daddio, whatever floats your boat."

He said, "Yopo."

I said, "Gesundheit."

He said, "No, friendo, it's what you need and I just so happen to have smuggled some back in a plastic bag up my butthole."

Hold the phone, butthole yopo? Yeah, no thanks, I told him. I was beaucoup skeptical until he explained. Yopo, otherwise known as Anadenanthera peregrina was prepared from the seeds of a tall forest tree. Once attained, the seeds were roasted gently and ground into a fine powder which, when mixed with an alkaline substance like leave ash, produced a violent hallucinogenic.

"It work through the skin?" I asked. "I don't think I'll be

able to slip him a Mickey Finn or anything."

"No problemo."

"And that yoyo stuff, it'll stay on a nickel?"

"It's 'yopo.'"

"Again, gesundheit. You should take some medicine for that cold of yours."

Stan thought about it and nodded. "I can figure something out."

"And he'll hallucinate?"

He went all wistful and wide-eyed with stripped-to-the-skivvies-in-the-jungle nostalgia. "Yeah. The lucky bastard."

After I scooped the nickels from the Brasher mansion, I hightailed it for Stan's pad. I'd told him not to make any plans for today and he'd listened. He said a batch of yopo was ready to roll and I handed over half the nickels. Half an hour later, it was done and I skedaddled, figuring if Janssen and his toughs were gonna track me down it would likely be at my abode. The depleted roll of nickels was in my pants pocket and the others were in a folded white envelope in my jacket. "You want to keep a level head," said Stan, as I walked away, "careful not to touch those."

So I knew the nickels packed a potent punch and wasn't too surprised when, after Butch went Splitsville and I cracked the joke about doggies loving cats, Reynold giggled. And stopped. And giggled some more

"What's so funny?" I asked, playing along.

"Butterflies," he said, swiping at the air above his head.

"No, Reynold, sorry. Those are bats."

His eyes went fear-wide. He panicked. He ducked down. He whipped his head back-and-forth. He tried to knife the bats circling his head. When that didn't work he ran off down the alley, screaming a high pitched sound I wouldn't have expected to come out of a no-neck tough guy like Reynold.

Janssen was on his own trip. He must've been hot because he'd already removed his jacket, tie and shirt. He was down to undershirt and pants and sweating profusely.

"Do you want to see the lights, Janssen?"

He nodded, slowly.

"This way." I led him out of the alley, to Hastings Street. The neon strip acid-bathed his eyeballs.

"Aaaaaaaaah," he said, probably seeing neon x 1000.

Noticing Reynold in the near distance, running along the sidewalk towards the Four Corners, I pointed. Best to keep the two as close to each other as possible for the inevitable clean up. I said, "That way, Copernicus." And he was okay to be compliant but he preferred to walk in the middle of the road, removing items of clothing as he went. Horns blared. Drivers cursed out of open windows.

I walked parallel to Janssen, on the sidewalk. With dusk safely in the rearview, the night was ready to play and Hastings Street wanted action. The spring air was crisp. The crowds milled on the sidewalk. Guys and gals. Ladies and gents. A six-car parade of horny teenage hot rod'ers cruised in cherry sleds and ogled any females whose attention they could grab with a horn toot and a corny wolf-whistle. There weren't many. The teens were acne-faced and testosterone-goofy.

Everyone stopped and stared at Janssen. He was down to his underwear now. Must've been sunny wherever he was. People clapped. They whistled. The teens and their hot rods carved a wide berth around him and kept driving.

Any other time and I would've been apt to stroll, to wander, to soak up the particular brand of magic that Hastings had to offer. Tonight, though, I had a job to do. Busted right hand throbbing something fierce, I stepped into the phone booth and closed the door.

18

— Hey, you remember me?
— Adora's mysterious caller returns.
— That's right. Hope you don't mind me tracking you down at work.
— No skin off my nose, bud. But the information ship has left the port. Smooth sailing ahead, all markers cleared.
— Consider this a little dinghy on its way to you, a one-way trip.
— I'm all ears.
— The widow Brasher and her chauffeur recently disappeared.
— You don't say.
— I do say. I'll also add there's a Rolls Royce trunk that doesn't smell very nice anymore, if you get my drift.
— That so?
— Unfortunately, yeah. Another thing I know is where the guy that put them in the trunk will be. If you were to send out a patrol car or seven after you hang

up you'd get your man.
— Sounds like a career maker.
— It is if you don't mind puttin' the handcuffs on a former police. See, Butch Montrose is your guy.
— No shit?
— No shit.
— Well, he was no friend of mine. And if we catch him red-handed I don't suppose anyone else will have a problem with it either.
— That's good because I'd also bet good money he's the reason some of your fellow boys in blue fished a corpse out of the Burrard Inlet last week. That body that got caught up in the trawler's net and ventilated with a blade so it wouldn't float.
— I heard something about that. Butch fell from grace hard, huh?
— Quick and without a parachute.
— Don't suppose you got an address.
— Don't suppose I do but it's in Shaughnessy, a few blocks north of 33rd. Think 'castle' and you'll find it.
— Ah, the Brasher estate. The plot thickens.
— That's the one.
— I know the place. They hosted a police charity ball a few years ago. Both of 'em gone now, eh? Damn shame. House was a little cramped for my taste, though. Could've used another wing, maybe an airport.
— Tell me about it. Okay, two more things and I'm outta your hair.
— Anything for the guy makin' my life easy street. Might get that promotion after all.
— You're gonna want to look up the phone number for the Kingston Psychiatric Hospital because you'll be

telling them soon you threw a net over a guy that jumped the fence at their facility a few years back.
— I will?
— I'd bet on it.
— Yeah, how much?
— Oh. I was thinkin' more a gentleman's bet.
— I see. That sure.
— But I do know somethin' for sure. Your desk is at the downtown station, right?
— You betcha.
— Well, your dispatch will be gettin' some calls pretty quick to come down to the Four Corners. There's a show going on.
— A show, eh? What do you mean? Buddy, hello?

— Hey, it's me.
— Hey, Me.
— Okay I called the restaurant?
— Special circumstances, Fitch.
— It's done.
— It worked?
— Like a charm.
— And our friend with the police was happy to oblige?
— More than. Gave him the skinny on Butch and where to find him and said there was a show nearby he should check out personally.
— And Janssen?
— Currently making quite a scene on Hastings and moving towards the Four Corners, so I'd say minutes from being scooped up.
— I have to hand it to you. Your plan came off.
— You sound shocked.

— Call it pleasantly surprised, with a hint of 'I knew you could do it'.
— I can live with that. Hey, that's—
— What?
— The tow rig just drove by. No mistaking it. Only one with my name on it.
— Ellie's there?
— Seems so.
— Oh no.
— What?
— I thought she only wanted it for protection so I didn't let her know I knew it was gone.
— What was gone?
— A .22 I keep in the closet. Well, kept. She snuck in there this morning. That's why when Ichabod asked me what he should do I said he should go. Told him to keep her safe. And to not shoot anybody.
— Well, they're here now.
— Fitch, that can't be good.
— Does she know Janssen had Rolly killed?
— I wouldn't put it past her.
— Would she do anything about it?
— Like you say about apples, Fitch…they don't tend to fall too far from the tree, do they?

19

I RAN. AS FAST AS I COULD. The sidewalk was crowded with pedestrians so I hopped off the curb and hit the street. Expecting gunfire any second made each second stretch over an eternity.

Water eroded rocks.

An ice age formed, melted, formed again.

By the time I'd snaked through the traffic jam of cars, the blaring horns, the people shouting various iterations of "What the bleep is going on up there?" Ellie had already stepped from cab of the tow truck, a few cars back from the Four Corners intersection. She strode forward, intent, right hand stuffed in her pocket.

"Ellie, no," I half-shouted. With cops on the way I didn't want to draw any attention to her. She didn't stop. I weaved and danced through traffic. I huffed and puffed up the slight rise to Main Street. I got struck by a car door opening, some square in a station wagon trying to get a better look at the issue. My broken hand screamed. I fought the scream down. I reached Ellie right as she stepped through the crosswalk.

My good hand on her shoulder, I gasped out a "Don't, please."

She turned, flushed, eyes afire. She was anger. She was revenge. She was packing the .22 in her leather jacket. I put my good hand to her wrist.

"No," I said. She tried to get her hand out of her pocket. I wouldn't let it.

"He deserves to die," she said, pointing to Janssen, who was stark naked and dancing in the middle of the intersection, waving his underwear around above his head.

"For that outfit, yes."

"Aren't you ever serious?"

"Not if I can help it. How'd you know?"

"I'm young, not stupid, Fitch. Why else would my mom be so interested in him? And I did a little digging around on my own. That mansion belongs to the Brasher family. A subsidiary of the Brasher family, Fell Brothers, Inc., purchased my father's tow truck business after his death."

"Thanks for telling me. I had to face off against a Knight of the Realm to get that far."

"It's called investigative work, Fitch, you should try it some time."

"Ouch."

The scene was getting crazier. A bus tried to get through the intersection but couldn't get around Janssen, who kept dancing and making unpredictable movements, and other cars tried to pass the bus, from each and every direction. Janssen was the hallucinating eye of a storm. An impatient driver tried to get around the bus and clipped Janssen on the hip. He ended up on the guy's hood.

Ellie repeated her thoughts on the matter.

"Yes," I said, "but it's not our place."

"What's that you always say: like mother, like daughter?"

"That's Adora's story and she's gotta live with the end. She doesn't want it to be yours. And neither do I."

Ellie stared at me. I stared back. I felt her grip on the pistol relax and I relaxed my grip on her wrist. Quid pro quo. When she pulled her hand out, no gun. I breathed again, not realizing I'd stopped. I reached into her pocket, palmed the tiny pistol and nodded for Ichabod, who'd followed behind me. He looked crestfallen by the lack of violence. I didn't know whose side he was really on and then realized once a Dead Clown always a Dead Clown. He may have been loyal to Adora and her daughter, but his true mistress was chaos.

Not today, clown. Not today.

Ichabod discreetly palmed the gun and walked away, moments before a swarm of cops rushed into the intersection. They secured the scene, stared down at Janssen writhing in agony/bliss on the ground and called for an ambulance, which arrived soon after.

As they loaded Janssen into the back of the ambulance, his fog cleared slightly and he spotted me watching from the edge of the crowd.

"That man there," he said. "I know him. Bring him to me."

The cops looked my way.

I looked around for the poor sap the nut on the stretcher was talking about.

A cop, a tall, rangy fellow, approached me. "You know this guy?" he asked.

"Nah," I said.

"Well, he thinks he knows you. Do you mind coming over? Maybe he says somethin' that helps us figure out what the hell is going on."

"Sure," I said, trying to keep it short. I was pretty sure this cop was Adora's contact, who I'd just spoken to on the phone, and I really didn't want to get recognized.

Sweat poured down Janssen's face. The jungle powder I

dosed him with had sent him straight into meltdown, a star going supernova. He looked rough, face locked in a grimace, like the pain from riding that car's hood was beginning to cut through the drug haze. He beckoned for me to lean in. I did. And he surprised me. His head was in the game. He had cards. He played cagey poker. He whispered words that chilled me to the bone. When he'd finished, I did my best to play it cool and stood up, shrugging my shoulders and shaking my head. Showbiz.

Janssen winked and grinned at me, at the world, as the paramedics finished loading him into the ambulance. When they slammed the doors shut, the cop pulled me aside, notebook at the ready. He asked me what Janssen said. I spun a tall tale and told him it was some nonsense about how he'd been to the jungle and brought back some "yoyo" or "yopo." The cop noted it down but was clearly disappointed. He escorted me back to the crowd, where Ellie waited. He thanked me and said we could return to our car. I turned to leave.

"Hold on a minute, fella," he said. He looked at the intersection, then back at me. "I noticed your hand. Looks swollen, maybe a few broken bones. You want me to have the medics take a look?"

"No thanks, officer. I don't want to be a bother."

"It's no trouble."

"Thanks but that won't be necessary."

"Okay, then, have it your way. Only tryin' to help out a good citizen. You are one, right?"

"I think so."

"I love the confidence. Still, I can't help but think maybe that car clipped you, too. Maybe your neck deep in this somehow. Maybe know more than you're sayin.'"

I held up my wreck of a hand. "What this? Unrelated." The cop. didn't look so sure. He sized me up for the umpteenth time. I said, "I slammed it in my car door just now."

"Yourself?"

"Yup, myself. I'm an idiot."

The cop looked to Ellie.

"He really is," she said, totally selling it.

20

AS I WAITED FOR THE DOC to cast my hand, the emergency room nurse, a saint if I ever met one, loaded a needle with painkiller like an airplane full of jet fuel and queued me up for take-off. At least the excruciating throbbing had subsided and my hand was only swollen if you thought a human hand shouldn't look bloated and puffy like a baseball mitt.

"Look on the bright side," I said to Adora, who'd met me at the hospital after Ichabod and Ellie dropped me off. Then Ichabod drove Ellie home and Adora stayed. "Put me in the outfield, nothing'll get by me."

"I was thinking more of getting the Circus of Cacophony sideshow back together. You could be the star attraction: 'Come one, come all. Behold the man with the mutant hand!'"

"That could work. Less running."

"Yes, there's that."

"Wipe that smirk off your face."

Adora played it cool, as always. "What smirk?"

"Right, sure."

"I'm not doing anything."

"No, you're not. It's almost worse. Say it. Get it over with."

"What?"

"That maybe this investigation biz ain't for me. Two cases, two hospital trips."

"What, really? I wasn't keeping track."

"Okay, uh huh."

"I've said what I have to say on that subject. At least this time you're not accusing me of murder."

"The night's young," I said, putting my head on her shoulder. She let me keep it there. "But I can't shake it."

"Shake what?"

"The feeling that Janssen was out there, lurking. Waiting for me for two years. Somehow, I set the whole twisted thing into motion."

She raised an eyebrow at me. "And who's got the God complex?"

"Oh, it's all a big coincidence?"

Adora conceded me that point. "Okay, maybe a bit of both. So, Janssen was removing the teeth of boozers and vagrants and replacing them with dentures while simultaneously drugging and brainwashing them to cure them of their vices?"

"He'd probably say 'custom drug cocktails that counteracted the patients' alcohol addictions so they can lead productive lives" but yeah. Though he had a special treatment for certain individuals, ones he could use, or that could serve him. Turned them into willing zombies from what I could see. And add to that list at least one wealthy 'benefactor', Hugo Brasher. Who knows, there may have been others. Lots of funerals out there. Or you simply create one. Janssen seemed to use a scattershot approach. Throw enough darts at the wall something will stick."

"That's why Rolly was killed. Janssen wanted his tow truck empire but he wouldn't sell. And Rolly was no Hugo Brasher. There'd be no drugging and enslaving that man."

"The tow truck was a clever angle, you think about it. Legit money coming in, a lot of it cash, so if you add some more and it's dirty it's a great place to clean it. And a roaming DSG sales force, helping out the distressed and depressed. A pamphlet here, a pamphlet there. It'd add up."

"But it still doesn't tell us why. To what end?"

I didn't answer. I didn't know. And Janssen knew it, too, and that's why he'd whispered those chilling words into my ear before being loaded into the ambulance:

"You have no idea, do you?" he'd said.

I thought about it now. Why does anyone do what they do? Money, power, fame. Short term, Janssen looked good to the outside world, helping to clean up skid row. New smile, new life. Bootstrap your own rebirth, that "teach a man to fish" kind of scam job. But long term, that's what killed me. I didn't know his big game, or if him being in custody even hurt it.

But I was caring less and less about anything, Janssen included, as my transatlantic flight taxied to the runway and was cleared for takeoff. Flight velocity achieved, I was pressed back into my seat. The nose lifted off the tarmac and minutes later I was soaring above the clouds, watching the emergency room waiting area from high. Far removed from the mystery and chaos of the world beneath me.

• • •

The Abbott Billiards Club was down a narrow stairwell off a small piece of Abbott Street real estate between the alley running parallel to the CN Railway tracks and Water Street.

The stairwell was familiar. Pretty sure I'd once believed it to be a muddy path from the forest leading into a glade populated by green-yellow skinned goblins playing a game involving sinking baby skulls down the gullets of adult skulls with their jaws pried unnaturally open. That, after I'd crossed over the void between worlds.

Then, it was drug-fueled hallucination, what Stanley called, "A trip, man."

Now, it was my nightmare, waking sweat-soaked and heart pounding.

I'd been retracing my steps from that night, in order to heal, to move on. And to see if there was any trace of Janssen and the DSG. There wasn't. The warehouse was deserted. I'd peered in through the window that Butch had shoved me out of but there was nothing to see. Only dust and emptiness. The whole place had been cleared out and I bet the propaganda drop had too. I went around back to the rear entrance and walked up the stairs in order to turn back around, look down. Anything to jog my memory in order to trace my steps from the night Janssen drugged me. I went back down the steps. I looked one way then the other. Right seemed more familiar so that's the way I went. I walked East for half-block until I came to the end of Abbott Street, where it jutted south. Across the street, on the other side of Abbott, there was a familiar staircase.

I'd been there before.

Once I reached the bottom of the staircase, I knew it to be true. The "glade" was actually a low-ceilinged pool hall and the tables the goblins played their game on was actually a very large billiards table. And, of course, the goblins were human beings playing billiards, just like how there were four gentlemen currently playing. And what an oddity I must've been to the players I stumbled across that night, a weirdo who'd crashed through the door then stood in the shadows and watched them.

I thought of the hallucinations, the goblin who'd spotted me and dragged me to his lair. I couldn't even begin to fathom what had actually transpired in real life until one of the gentleman playing billiards stopped, carefully laid his cue on the green felt of a neighbouring table and approached me.

It was him, the goblin. Except now, he was a mid-fifties guy, scrappy, solidly built, dressed well in brown slacks, a tweed coat and a flat cap. He spoke. I understood nothing. It took a while. It sunk in. Oh. What I thought of that wild night as goblin-speak was actually a thick Irish brogue.

I said my name was Fitch. His said his name was Joe. We shook hands. He asked how I'd been. I told him it'd been an interesting couple of weeks and he agreed it must have.

"Lad, you were right fucked that night. Outta your skull."

"Yes, I was."

"Aye, you thought I was a goblin."

"I said that, did I? Sorry."

"Think nothing of it. But I didn't know what else to do so I thought it best to get you somewhere you could sleep it off. Then I thought, well, every man needs to look good even if he thinks I'm a monster."

"Can you take a break from your game of pool and show me?"

"Snooker, lad. And I can."

Joe led me to his barbershop, which was on Water Street, equidistant from both the Abbott Billiards Club and the warehouse. The shop had a snazzy tile floor, framed black-and-white photos of Joe's Irish homeland on the wall, and the obligatory spinning barber's pole outside. I had to laugh when I saw the chair and figured it out.

"I thought you were going to slit my throat but it was a shave, wasn't it?"

"Aye. Had to strap you down with my belt and bit of old rope from the cellar so you'd settle."

I felt my face, the stubble there. "Guess it grew out by the time I was thinking straight again, so I didn't notice. But the haircut I did. Nice work." I offered to pay him for his service. He waved his hand, no.

"That one was on the house. Next one you pay for."

"Deal."

"Where'd you end up, lad? You ran out of here screaming like a bog banshee as soon as I took the restraints off."

"Kitsilano beach, covered in sand and bird shit."

Joe laughed and patted my shoulder in brotherhood. "Had a few nights like that myself, haven't I?"

• • •

The guy at the framing store was early-20s with a duckbill haircut and Buddy Holly specs. He looked prepared to be mucho unimpressed by anything anyone over 25 would have to say. That is until I showed him what I had. His eyes bugged out. He went, "Woah." He thought it had to be a joke, walking around with a signed cheque like that. Not only did it look like the paper version of Frankenstein's monster, all taped up and cobbled together, but all those zeros.

"That's not real is it?" he asked.

"You think a guy like me gets a cheque like that? Nah, it's a joke among friends."

"Nice friends, daddio."

"Well, maybe acquaintances. Daddio."

After I paid, he said it would be an hour and walked away shaking his head, still looking at the cheque. Probably imagining everything he could do with dough like that. Buy a cherry sled. Get some new threads. Pick up a guitar. Start a band. Cut a record. Play some shows. Get girls. Get famous. Get more girls. I knew how he felt. Minus the guitar and the band, but including the girls, it was everything I'd once imagined I could do with a pile of cash.

When the cheque was done and framed, I went back to my room to hang it near the door. Hammering in a nail using my left hand was not easy but I got the job done and the frame hid the holes I bashed in the wall in the process. I'd dug through the garbage in the Brasher study to collect the paper scraps right after snatching my roll of nickels off the desk but before luring Mr. Jangles into my arms using an opened can of tuna I found in the pantry.

I couldn't pass up the opportunity for a keepsake. Now, every day I could look at the cheque and say to myself, Okay, I might still be living in a one-room apartment in a boarding house for ne'er do wells and down-and-outs and treat a dive diner like both office and living room, but I still had a few principles that couldn't be bought.

What could be bought for me was sympathy diner coffee and I soaked up every drop I could get. My hand cast was a hit and the story about how it happened changed depending on the diner denizen you talked to. I neither confirmed nor denied and enjoyed the ambiguity, even if others didn't. But I wasn't about to loop myself in with anything nefarious that had occurred that night with Janssen, Reynold or Butch. That was a can of worms best left unopened because the police were neck deep in Janssen's business and getting out the scuba diving suits. Bodies and headlines tended to do that.

I read about the scene at the Brasher mansion in the newspaper. Summoned to the estate by an anonymous caller complaining about "strange noises," the cops found Kathleen Brasher and her chauffeur, Seamus Kelly, in the trunk of a Rolls Royce belonging to the Brasher family. Mrs. Brasher died of strangulation, while Mr. Kelly bled to death from several knife wounds. Skin under both victims' nails revealed their attacker to be Butch Montrose, a former police officer turned private security consultant. Mr. Montrose had also been found dead at the scene, stabbed to death by an antique sword. Hugo Brasher, found clutching the sword, had been arrested for the murder of Butch Montrose, though the family's attorney was already claiming self-defense.

"That sure is something, eh, Fitch?" Glenda was hovering over my shoulder.

"Sure is."

"Bunch of lunatics out there."

"Tell me about it." I raised my hand cast. "And I manage to keep runnin' afoul of them."

"Lucky, eh?"

"That's one way of lookin' at it."

Glenda laughed, reached down under the counter for a marker and wrote in big block letters, ONE LUCKY GUY, across my cast, roughly where my knuckles were. She also added a few hearts and signed her name so that made me feel better. After she'd walked away, shaking her head at the madness in the world, I kept reading the newspaper.

The same night they found Butch's body in Shaughnessy, another suspect in Kathleen Brasher and Seamus Kelly's death was picked up by the police in downtown Vancouver. Reynold Dietz, found with the knife suspected in the murder of Mr. Kelly, was arrested on Saturday evening at the Four Corners and was currently undergoing psychiatric evaluation. Also taken into custody that evening was one Copernicus Janssen, who was causing a disturbance only a few blocks from where Dietz was arrested. Janssen escaped from the Kingston Psychiatric Hospital in 1955 and was also known locally as Quincy Quest, the leader of the Disciples of the Sacred Glow, an organization that helped skid row denizens get back on their feet. He was being held for observation and questioning to determine his part, if any, in the recent killings.

Fitch, you wily operator, I thought to myself. Had to admit, I was proud for guessing correctly that Janssen was a booby hatch escapee. Pure instinct. But as my mother always said, even a broken clock is right twice a day. My victory felt anticlimactic and short lived when I imagined the police interrogation like Janssen dancing on ice. He'll twist. He'll twirl. He'll skate free from any accusations like he was born in an ice rink with sharp blades for feet.

Reynold, though, didn't seem very graceful to me and would probably land on his ass. Still, I didn't want to leave it up to chance, so the last thing I did before leaving the diner was amble to the phone near the kitchen and make another anonymous call to the cops. Told them a little birdie whispered in my ear that Reynold Dietz was seen at the health club the morning Rolly Stevens ended up in a coma and it might be worth a look-see…especially since Butch Montrose investigated and wasn't ol' Butch an ex-cop murderer and now dead as a doornail after being impaled by a sword?

I didn't have enough to box up Janssen for delivery so I left him out of it. He had a warrant out for escaping from Kingston Psychiatric Hospital so I figured that had to be good for a few months of three-squares and a cot at the government's expense. Maybe I could dig something up on him, glue that would stick.

Or maybe not.

Like with my run-in with the Dead Clowns and all that

verbal sparring with Adora Carmichael last year, there were a lot of maybes floating around in the air these days.

Like maybe Janssen, when he was lying on the ambulance stretcher, eyes gleaming with mischief, drug sweat beading on his forehead like he'd been waxed with a layer of Carnuba, didn't really whisper in my ear.

You have no idea, do you?

But I knew that he had.

And maybe I didn't really see the faces I recognized from Gastown—the same ones I'd also seen at the warehouse, beginning their "therapy" with the DSG—around town these days. But I knew that I did, though not behind dumpsters in the alleys and propping up bar stools in my local. No, in actual jobs. Always clean shaven and big of teeth, new dentures sparkling. Waiting tables in restaurants bartending at snooty bars where lawyers and judges frolicked. Pushing luggage carts from outside fancy cars to inside fancy hotels. Climbing up poles to fix bum telephone lines.

Always relatively menial, but insider positions.

Close to infrastructure. Close to power, the wealthy, the movers and shakers.

They were infiltrating. They were gaining access to the network of things, becoming intertwined in society's guts.

Or maybe not.

Maybe I was a paranoid loon.

Maybe I was full of shit.

21

BILLY ANSWERED THE DOOR, even ganglier than the last time I saw him. Didn't know it was possible, like surely his body must have reached a pact with the invading force of testosterone by now. Apparently not and he was long-of-limb, acne-cheeked, broken-voiced and all with the faint wisp of a cheesy mustache on his upper lip. Puberty had him by the scruff of the neck and was not letting go. Not yet. Too much fun was being had at Billy's expense.

"Fitch?" he said, eyeing me, then the blanket-covered box at my feet. "What're you doing here?"

"Got a surprise for you." I took the blanket off the cat carrier and lifted it up to Billy. I may have failed Kathleen Brasher, her son, Hugo, and the chauffeur but not this kid. "It's Mr. Jangles."

Billy went green in the gills. He looked back into the house. He moved forward onto the welcome mat and closed the door behind him. Not the reaction I expected. I thought more excitement, maybe some confetti. After all, Fitch had done it, come through, done him a solid and found his missing cat, against all odds. But no. He said, "You gotta go, Fitch. And take the cat with you."

"But Billy…"

"Mr. Jangles is inside."

I looked into the cage. The cat meowed. It was definitely Mr. Jangles. "I think you're wrong on that. Look at the tag."

"No, you don't get it. My Mr. Jangles is inside right now. See, my mom was so sad when her boyfriend left. Then the cat ran away. Butch was a deadbeat, couldn't help that, but I could do something about Mr. Jangles. So I took the money I'd had saved up from my paper route and found a calico at the pet shelter that looked enough like Mr. Jangles to fool my mom, who actually doesn't like cats that much. I just didn't want her to be sad that I was sad, you know? So don't blow my cover, okay?"

Billy was scared. His eyes pleaded. Single mom heartbreak and a kid trying to mop up the spill. It hit home. It rang memory bells. I could relate. I sympathized with his cause. Not an easy road for him ahead, as there was always another spill, another mess, but he'd have to figure that out for himself. Decide his own level of involvement. I vowed to myself to check in now-and-then, make sure everything was as copacetic as possible.

"Sure," I said, nodding. "You got it, Billy. Me and this cat, we're ghosts."

My new feline friend didn't waste any time in making himself at home. Within an hour of being in my room, the cat formerly known as Mr. Jangles had torn up my pillow and scratched up the door. But he'd also killed a mouse and batted a cockroach back-and-forth in its paws like a hockey puck.

"Cat," I said, "you're hired. I pay in canned tuna and kitty litter. What do you say?"

The cat did its leg-splay-and-crotch-lick routine.

I took that as a yes.

• • •

The nightmares continued, morphing, changing. As the weeks went by, the hallucination flashbacks about goblins and voids faded, only to be replaced by realizations made at painkiller cruising altitude. Though I couldn't figure out if it was my own brain that conjured them up or if it had been Adora telling me, there in the emergency room waiting room.

You're stuck in a loop, Fitch.

You're going around and around.

Think about it: get a half-baked 'case' and make a half-baked investigation. Run into some bad people, some good people and some crazy people. End up in the hospital. Kind of figure some stuff out but not really. All the while flirting with a diner waitress and drinking diner coffee.

You're a satellite in orbit, rotating, observing.

Your orbit won't change until you figure out what you should be doing. New trajectories.

And sure, you'll add a few people to your orbit each time, maybe a dog next time, another pal, carve a bigger path, but a circle's a circle no matter how big.

The end becomes the beginning.

And the next go-round might kill you.

Ever think of that?

So, what's the real question?

What's your mystery?

Who really left you?

What won't you admit to anyone, even yourself?

What really happened to your mother?

When you got back from your hobo life, from running away, where did she go without a trace? No forwarding address left, no word whatsoever.

Isn't that your missing person?

The BIG CASE you always wanted.

You're stuck in a loop, Fitch.

You're going around and around and—

Always woke up sweating, heart pounding, gasping, brain swirling with new, even scarier, goblins: the truth, the lies, and everything in-between.

— Ellie?
— Yeah?
— It's Fitch.
— No shit.
— Language.
— Go fly a kite, daddio.
— Your eloquence is inspiring.
— You call for a reason?
— I did. You still want to show me how the tow game works?
— I don't know. You gonna be a good student?
— All the coffee and apples a teacher can handle.
— I'll think about it.
— I can live with that.

— Hello?
— Hi. This Wendell?
— Yeah.
— Tall fella, fists like anvils?
— I suppose. What's it to ya?

— Finally. I had to call every mining company in the book to find you.
— That right? I owe you money or somethin'?
— No, other way around.
— Heh?
— Do you remember a daytime bar brouhaha you got into a few years ago in Toronto? A little fisticuff with a well-dressed handsome fella that ended in a handshake and pat on the shoulder?
— Nah. I only punch losers.
— Funny.
— Flinch, wasn't it? I remember. I bought you a beer and you lifted my nickels.
— I did. Apologies. Not very neighbourly.
— You called to tell me that?
— It's been weighin' on me.
— Ah, don't sweat it. Those nickels only brought me grief, you look at it a certain way. Made me more likely to punch my way out of trouble than not. How'd they do for you?
— Oh, like a charm, Wendell. Went straight to the track and put that two bucks on a horse that paid out 10-1. Then those winnings on a horse that paid out 50-1. People started noticing me after that so I started charging for my betting advice. Set up a little bookie shop and the phone rang day and night. Made a pretty penny. Then a publisher approached me to write a book, go legit, and I called it "Horses for Courses" and it sold a bunch of copies. Now I'm sittin' on Easy Street.
— Flinch, you magnificent bastard. How about cuttin' me in on a piece of the action for my initial investment. Hello? Flinch?

Acknowledgments

Thanks to all the creative influences that got me this far. Your work and spirit resonates. Most of all, thanks to my family and friends for the continued support. You keep me pushing. Now, please stop reading and go out and tell someone to buy this book. A writer gotta eat.

Photo by Charles Lester

R. DANIEL LESTER writes into the void. Sometimes the void wins. Other times the words win. Over the years, his work has appeared in multiple publications, including Shotgun Honey, Bareknuckles Pulp, The Flash Fiction Offensive, Switchblade, Retreats from Oblivion and the clown noir anthology, *Greasepaint & 45s*. His novella, *Dead Clown Blues*, was nominated by the Crime Writers of Canada for a 2018 Arthur Ellis Award. Previously a longtime Vancouver resident, he currently lives in Toronto with his spouse and daughter. The battle with the void continues daily.

DOWN & OUT BOOKS

On the following pages are a few
more great titles from the
Down & Out Books publishing family.

For a complete list of books and to
sign up for our newsletter,
go to **DownAndOutBooks.com**.

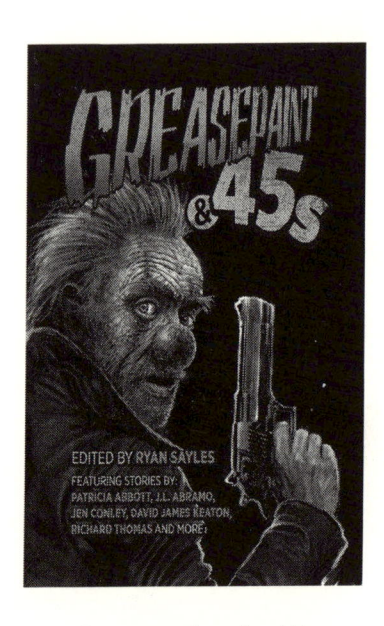

Greasepaint & .45s
Edited by Ryan Sayles

Down & Out Books
May 2019
978-1-948235-85-3

Clowns are like politics; everyone has an opinion on them.
In this collection of short stories you'll find numerous takes on the world of the painted harlequin entertainer. Often maligned in today's day and age, the institution of the clown means something to everyone.

Edited by Ryan Sayles and featuring stories by Patricia Abbott, J.L. Abramo, Jen Conley, Jeffery Hess, Grant Jerkins, David James Keaton, Ed Kurtz, R. Daniel Lester, Marietta Miles, Warren Moore, Chuck Regan, Scotch Rutherford, Liam Sweeney, Richard Thomas, James R. Tuck, and Lono Waiwaiole.

Dead Clown Blues
A Carnegie Fitch Mystery Fiasco
R. Daniel Lester

Shotgun Honey, an imprint of
Down & Out Books
September 2017
978-1-946502-02-5

Carnegie Fitch, once-upon-a-time drifter and now half-assed private eye, has a sharp tongue, a cheap suit and dog-bite marks on his fedora. Yes, that's just how he rolls through the downtown streets of Vancouver, BC, aka Terminal City, circa 1957, a land of neon signs, 24-hour diners and slumming socialites. And on the case of a lifetime, a case of the dead clown blues.

Strangers in a Strange Land
Immigrant Stories
Edited by Chris Rhatigan and Katherine Tomlinson

All Due Respect, an imprint of
Down & Out Books
January 2019
978-1-64396-008-1

Strangers in a Strange Land: Immigrant Stories is an anthology that explores immigration in poems, essays, and short stories by a diverse collection of authors who offer their own experiences, observations, and speculations. From searing poetry drawn from a Native American perspective to essays chronicling the marginalization of LGBT people, to the crime fiction of new Americans and writers whose ancestors were brought to the country in bondage, this collection examines the intersection of hope and despair that defines the immigrant experience.

Once a World
Craig McDonald

Down & Out Books
July 2019
978-1-64396-026-5

Welcome to America, circa 1916-1918, and two of the bloodiest conflicts that starkly defined an era.

Teenage Hector Lassiter, an aspiring author inspired by propaganda and a siren's song of throbbing war drums, lies about his age, mounts a horse, and storms across the Mexican border behind General "Black Jack Pershing" and George S. Patton to bring the terrorist and Revolutionary General Pancho Villa to justice.

Soon, Hector is shipped off to the bloody trenches of France, fighting the so-called "War to End All Wars" where he meets fellow novelists-in-waiting, John Dos Passos and Ernest Hemingway.